THE SILENT WATCHER

Bart Shallock, smoothest confidence man in New York, was on to something—millions of dollars. That's what he would get if his hired mobsters could muscle in on some big money that was meant for good causes. The boss said so, and the boss should know. He was none other than the brilliant archcriminal known as "Crix"!

What Bart Shallock didn't know was that someone was standing in the room with him at that very moment, watching and listening to all his evil plans, waiting in silence for the moment when Shallock, "Crix," and all their minions would come face to face with a dark-cloaked, gleaming-eyed figure armed with the blazing guns of justice.

When would that moment come? *The Shadow knew!*

Maxwell Grant was the pen-name adopted by Walter B. Gibson to recount the adventures of a mysterious crime fighter known as The Shadow, who frequently appeared as Lamont Cranston, wealthy man about-town. Over a period of 15 years, Gibson wrote more than 275 novel-length stories of The Shadow which appeared exclusively in The Shadow Magazine and formed the basis for the popular radio series, which featured Lamont Cranston as The Shadow.

Published by
Pyramid Books:

THE LIVING SHADOW—SHADOW #1
THE BLACK MASTER—SHADOW #2
MOBSMEN ON THE SPOT—SHADOW #3
HANDS IN THE DARK—SHADOW #4
DOUBLE Z—SHADOW #5
THE CRIME CULT—SHADOW #6
THE RED MENACE—SHADOW #7
MOX—SHADOW #8
THE ROMANOFF JEWELS—SHADOW #9
THE SILENT SEVEN—SHADOW #10
KINGS OF CRIME—SHADOW #11
THE SHADOWED MILLIONS—SHADOW #12
GREEN EYES—SHADOW #13
THE CREEPING DEATH—SHADOW #14
GRAY FIST—SHADOW #15
THE SHADOW'S SHADOW—SHADOW #16
FINGERS OF DEATH—SHADOW #17

Murder Trail

FROM THE SHADOW'S PRIVATE ANNALS

as told to

MAXWELL GRANT

A JOVE/HBJ BOOK

Published by arrangement with The Condé Nast Publications, Inc.

First Jove/HBJ edition published October 1977
Originally published in THE SHADOW Magazine, Volume 5, #2, March 15, 1933

Library of Congress Catalog Card Number: 77-83158

Printed in the United States of America

Jove/HBJ books are published by Jove Publications, Inc.
(Harcourt Brace Jovanovich)
757 Third Avenue, New York, N.Y. 10017

CHAPTER I

THE STOWAWAY

Heinrich Von Werndorff, captain of the *Munchen,* was seated at the tiny desk in his cabin aboard the mammoth dirigible. The big airship was resting in its hangar at Friedrichshafen. From the window of the cabin, the captain could see the gloomy ground below, where occasional workmen passed back and forth. This was the night before the air liner's scheduled voyage.

Captain von Werndorff was nervous. That was quite unusual. A veteran of numerous transatlantic flights, now commander of the newest and most air-worthy dirigible that had ever been constructed, there was no apparent reason for Von Werndorff to be apprehensive. Nevertheless, the captain's heavy-jowled face wore a serious expression that indicated anxiety.

A rap at the door of the cabin. Von Werndorff swung in his chair. In a low, guttural tone, he ordered the visitor to come in. A young man, trim in uniform, entered and saluted with military procedure. This was Lieutenant Fritz von Salzburg, second in command aboard the *Munchen.*

Von Werndorff watched while his subordinate closed the door of the cabin. The lieutenant approached and leaned upon the table, to whisper these words close in the commander's ear:

"The man has arrived, Herr Captain."

"Where is he?" came Von Werndorff's tense question. "You are sure that no one has seen him?"

"He has been unobserved, Herr Captain. I met him

at the appointed place. I brought him aboard the dirigible. He is waiting in the corridor.

Von Werndorff gave a relieved sigh. With a kindly commendation that one would not have expected from so stern an individual, he clapped his brawny hand upon the lieutenant's back, and spoke in a tone that was almost fatherly.

"Excellent, Fritz," he said, "excellent! You will show the visitor in, and then leave the ship. Wait below, and make sure that no one comes aboard. Above all, Fritz, remember——"

"My lips are closed, Herr Captain."

A full minute passed, while Captain von Werndorff drummed upon the table. Again, the door of the cabin opened, and a short, heavy-set figure entered. This was the visitor—a man whose face could not be seen within the huge collar of the coat which he was wearing.

The visor of a large cap was over the man's forehead; but when he saw that the captain sat alone, the visitor threw aside the cap and turned down his collar.

Von Werndorff, rising, stood with his huge bulk at attention. His stern face was impassive, while his eyes gazed toward the solemn, haughty countenance of the shorter man before him.

A quiet smile appeared upon the visitor's lips. The man motioned the commander to his chair, and took a seat beside the table.

"All is prepared?" he questioned, in an even voice.

"Yes, your excellency," responded the captain.

"Good," said the visitor, in a tone of satisfaction. "I knew that I could rely upon you, Von Werndorff."

The commander bowed in acknowledgment. He had flown Zeppelins during the period of the War; and this man had been his superior then. Captain Von Werndorff was loyalty personified. He had not forgotten.

"Baron Hugo von Tollsburg," the captain began

a low-voiced statement, "I shall always obey your orders——"

The visitor stopped Von Werndorff with an imperious gesture. He smiled wanly, and slowly shook his head as the captain became silent.

"Baron von Tollsburg is no more," he said quietly. "The old regime is forgotten. Peace, not war, is my mission to-day. I told you that, Von Werndorff, when I visited you months ago, at the time when this great ship was in course of construction."

"I remember," nodded the commander.

"You promised then," resumed the visitor, "to make the arrangements that I requested. I relied upon you—although I was not to see you until this night, the eve of your voyage to America. I am here, captain. I am ready. Let us go; it is unwise to remain in this cabin."

Von Werndorff sprang to his feet. He opened the door of the cabin and beckoned to the visitor. Von Tollsburg followed him along the corridor. On each side of the narrow passage were doorways; and here, in the gloom of lights set far apart, the great gondola of the dirigible seemed as cavernous as the interior of an ocean steamship.

With accommodations for more than one hundred persons, the *Munchen* was an air liner of mammoth dimensions, and Von Tollsburg, here for the first time, appreciated its great size to the full.

Captain von Werndorff stopped as he neared the end of the corridor. He was at a space where two doors on the left stood a full six feet apart. The same was true on the right. This section of the ship bore the appearance of a strengthening bulkhead.

The visitor watched in admiration as Captain von Werndorff drew a picklike instrument and ran it down the crevice at one side of the space between the doors. A muffled click occurred. The metal wall swung outward. The captain stood back and motioned his visitor to enter.

Von Tollsburg walked into a pitch black room. The commander followed him; a click came, and the two were confined within the bulkhead.

Captain von Werndorff ran his hand along the wall, and a tiny light suddenly gleamed. It illuminated the room in which the two were standing. A small, windowless chamber, this was a secret room aboard the dirigible—a spot that no one would possibly have suspected.

"This is the apartment, your excellency," said Von Werndorff, with a bow. "It is small; but I have spared no pains to make it habitable."

He probed the farther wall with his pick. A small closet opened. Von Werndorff revealed shelves stocked with canned goods.

"This serves two purposes," he explained. "It carries your supplies. It is also a ventilating shaft. Up here——" he pointed to an opening at the side of the closet——" is communication with the berth in the wall. Air is always there. Keep the closet door open during your waking hours——when you sleep, there is no need of worry."

Then, stepping back, Von Werndorff pointed to the wall, and marked a crevice with his fingers.

"Two catches hold the berth," he explained. "You will find no difficulty in operating it. I promised, your excellency, that you would be comfortable aboard my ship."

"A stowaway de luxe," responded Von Tollsburg, with a smile.

"Exactly," acknowledged the commander.

"And as for America?" the visitor questioned.

"Our destination is Chicago," declared Von Werndorff. "Weather conditions should be perfect. We shall arrive on schedule. I shall insist upon a thorough inspection of the ship for my own protection. After that, your departure will be easy. I shall arrange all."

Hugo von Tollsburg extended his hand. The dirigible

commander seized it warmly. The two men faced each other as sworn friends.

"Von Werndorff," said the baron, in a tone that was low, but clear, "you have cooperated with me to perfection. When I visited you months ago, and told you that I wished to travel to America unbeknown, you agreed to my plan without question. You provided this secret place for my passage.

"I am ready for the voyage. I feel confident that all will occur as I have planned. These words are my farewell. I shall not speak again. When we arrive in the United States, come to this cabin and announce when the path is clear."

"I shall obey," responded the commander.

"Remember this," added Von Tollsburg. "No one must ever know that Hugo von Tollsburg was aboard this airship. My mission is tremendously important. It must be preserved a secret. That is your only duty now.

"Whatever may occur in the future is my affair alone. Not one bit of evidence should remain to indicate that I came on board. You understand?"

"I understand."

"Should you need aid in removing me from this airship, rely only upon your trusted lieutenant; but give him no word as to my identity. A great work is at stake, Von Werndorff. Secrecy is paramount."

"I shall never speak."

The interview was ended.

Alone, Baron Hugo von Tollsburg breathed a sigh of relief. He could feel the draft of cool air coming through the ventilator that connected with the opened closet.

He was a stowaway aboard the *Munchen*. To-morrow, the great airship would be crowded with passengers for the transatlantic flight—and with them, hidden beyond all chance of discovery, would be a mysterious stowaway, hidden in a secret chamber cunningly contrived for his reception.

Von Tollsburg drew a large envelope from the pocket of his coat. The man's firm face, impassive even to the pointed tips of his military mustache, showed plainly as it came close to the light. From the envelope, Von Tollsburg removed a stack of American currency and a sheaf of folded papers.

A stern smile flickered over Von Tollsburg's well-formed lips. The baron's cold, gray eyes made a careful inspection of the articles from the envelope. With satisfaction, Von Tollsburg pocketed his possessions. He closed the door of the hidden closet, and stood in the center of the secret room.

Completely isolated from the world without; protected by sound-proof walls, Baron von Tollsburg was ready for the long and secret flight that would carry him, unheralded, halfway across the American continent. Smuggled here by the captain of the Zeppelin, he was confident that he had reached the safety zone in the mission that he had undertaken.

He did not dread the journey. Calm and unperturbed, he planned for sleep. He found the crevice that indicated the berth in the wall, and inserted the pick. Catches clicked; the berth swung downward on noiseless hinges, to reveal the blackened space that received its air from the ventilator shaft.

As Von Tollsburg leaned forward toward the berth, a low, guttural gasp came from his lips. His hands shot upward in a mad effort to ward off unexpected danger. His body writhed furiously, casting long, twisting shadows in the dim light of the secret cabin.

The gasp had ended unheard; in its place came a choking gargle that slowly toned away to a harsh rattle.

Half drawn into the blackness of the berth, Von Tollsburg's body became motionless. It moved backward, as though impelled by an unseen force. It stood grotesquely, supported by a hidden grasp. Then, released, it toppled and crumpled upon the floor.

Buried within the secret cabin, the form of Baron Hugo von Tollsburg lay inert and lifeless. The stowaway aboard the dirigible *Munchen* had met with a cruel and unexpected fate. His mission had ended before the flight had begun!

CHAPTER II

THE SHADOW OBSERVES

The dirigible *Munchen* was nearing the last leg of its westward flight. Its huge bulk gliding onward, the mammoth airship rode with marvelous stability. Purring motors kept up their constant rhythm. The passengers in the forward salon smiled and chatted as the Zeppelin whirred through the night.

Dawn would arrive within a few hours. Gleaming rays of sunlight would show the silver queen of the air entering the fringe of the Middle West. The Atlantic had been conquered; the rest of the voyage offered no obstacles.

Captain Heinrich von Werndorff entered the salon. His arrival brought words of commendation from the group of men who saw him. The commander bowed at the congratulations.

"We are experiencing great success," he declared. "This voyage, gentlemen, is a triumph for the dirigible as a means of transportation. With our destination an inland city, instead of a seaport, we are proving the advantages of air liners over ocean liners."

He caught the eye of a gentleman seated in a corner of the salon, and smiled as though in mutual congratulation.

"You were fortunate, Herr Arnaud," said the captain. "Your last-minute arrival at Friedrichshafen enabled you to join us on this memorable voyage. You came as a good omen."

All turned toward the man to whom the commander

had spoken. Henry Arnaud had been regarded as an unusual passenger on this flight. He had made reservation by wire from Moscow, and had reached the Friedrichshafen hangar just as the *Munchen* was about to sail.

There was something about Henry Arnaud's appearance that commanded both respect and interest. Although an American, he spoke fluently in French, German, and Russian, and had thus made an acquaintance with passengers of those nationalities.

Captain von Werndorff was speaking in German as he addressed Arnaud; and the American replied in the same language.

"The good omen on the *Munchen,*" he said, in a quiet tone, "is the presence of our commander, Captain von Werndorff."

A buzz of approval was the response to the compliment. Henry Arnaud, calm-faced and impassive in demeanor, was a man who spoke with profound sincerity. His eyes, sharp and piercing, were gazing toward Von Werndorff, and the commander noted the strange sparkle that came from them. Somehow, he felt that those eyes had stared at him before.

The passengers, now that the United States had been reached, were preparing to retire. They were leaving the salon one by one; and Henry Arnaud was among the last to go. His eyes gave a parting glance toward Von Werndorff; the commander, acting under impulse, reached forward and plucked the American's sleeve.

"Herr Arnaud," he said, in German, "I do not recall having met you in the past; yet there is something in your manner that indicates you have seen me before."

A slight smile played upon Arnaud's thin lips. The man's expression was sphinxlike. His burning eyes gleamed upon Von Werndorff. The commander was amazed when Arnaud spoke.

"This is not my first voyage with you, captain," he

said in a low voice. "I have seen you before; and then, as now, I was aboard a ship of yours."

"You mean——"

"During the War, Herr Captain. You will recall"——Arnaud's eyes were sparkling——" a dirigible flight across the North Sea, when a storm drove you back to Germany. That storm proved fortunate, Herr Captain; fortunate for both of us. My mission was to see that the Zeppelin did not reach England."

"You were aboard the L-43!"

"Yes."

"As a member of the crew?"

"As a stowaway."

"As a stowaway!"

When he repeated Arnaud's word, Captain von Werndorff's face became momentarily pale. Perhaps it was the memory of that eventful war flight over the North Sea; or was there another reason for the commander's loss of color?

Henry Arnaud noted the captain's change of expression, and added a brief statement that might have ordinarily been a simple explanation. As chance had it, the words brought a new and more singular turn to Von Werndorff's complexion.

"Your superior came aboard the L-43," reminded Arnaud. "An aid accompanied him. The aid did not leave. He became a stowaway. A simple ruse, Herr Captain, but it worked. It deceived both you and your superior——Baron Hugo von Tollsburg."

It was the mention of this name that made Von Werndorff repress a gasp. Out of the past had come a series of coincidences. This man had been a stowaway on the L-43. He had come aboard that ship with Von Tollsburg.

Now, by a curious reversal of circumstances, Baron von Tollsburg was a stowaway on the *Munchen,* while Henry Arnaud was the passenger!

Was there a connection here? Was Henry Arnaud a

man whom Baron von Tollsburg sought to avoid? Perplexities swept through the commander's brain; then he regained his poise as Henry Arnaud made a quiet parting remark.

"I am glad to travel with you again, Herr Captain," said the American. "It is a pleasure to be a passenger aboard your dirigible. Stowaways aboard Zeppelins once could have expected death if discovered. In these times of peace, they receive reasonable treatment. It is preferable, however, to be a listed passenger."

Arnaud extended his hand to Von Werndorff, and the dirigible commander received it. The American turned and left the salon.

Von Werndorff remained thoughtful. With chin in hand, he did not realize that Arnaud's sharp gaze had caught his immediate reaction.

It was coincidence, Von Werndorff felt sure, that had brought this man aboard the *Munchen* as a passenger. Arnaud's remarks could have been nothing more than a friendly revelation of the past. In this surmise, the commander was correct.

But Von Werndorff made the mistake of discounting his own reactions. He did not realize that his stern face, by its betrayal of emotions, had spoken to Henry Arnaud as effectively as if words had been uttered. Here, above the United States, speeding toward the end of the oceanic flight, Henry Arnaud had gained the remarkable suspicion that there was a mystery aboard this airship!

After he left the main salon, the commander of the *Munchen* still felt a trace of uneasiness. He went into his cabin and consulted a passenger list. He learned the number of Henry Arnaud's cabin—28. Passing along the narrow central corridor, Von Werndorff paused at the door which bore that number.

He satisfied himself that all was quiet within. Henry Arnaud had evidently retired.

With only a slight apprehension remaining, Von Werndorff continued along the corridor.

As he walked toward the rear of the great gondola, something happened behind him. The door of Henry Arnaud's cabin opened, and a pair of gleaming eyes watched the commander's course.

Those eyes saw Captain von Werndorff pause beside a bulkhead on the left, and listen there intently. When the commander came back along the corridor, Henry Arnaud was no longer watching him.

Smoothly, the *Munchen* plowed on through the night. Within Cabin 28, Henry Arnaud stood by the door, listening. The cabin light clicked on; the American stooped above his berth. His form was suddenly lost amid a shrouding robe of black. A few moments later, Henry Arnaud was gone; and in his place stood a strange and fantastic being.

A tall, mysterious figure, garbed in black; this was the personage into which Henry Arnaud had transformed himself. The folds of a sable-hued cloak enveloped his body; the broad brim of a dark slouch hat obscured his visage. Henry Arnaud had become The Shadow!

A soft laugh that came from unseen lips announced the identity of the mysterious figure. The low tones of that sinister mockery were inimitable. No other living person could have uttered them.

The Shadow, who hounded criminals of every land, had booked passage aboard the *Munchen* in his adopted guise of Henry Arnaud. By chance, he had learned that Captain von Werndorff was harboring a secret. He had divined the presence of a stowaway aboard this dirigible. He had aroused the commander's apprehensions, and had caused Von Werndorff to visit the secret spot where the stowaway was hidden.

Now, as a phantom shape, The Shadow was about to investigate the situation. With his penchant for unraveling meshes of mystery, he intended to learn more of the matter which now concerned him. The actions of the captain needed much explanation.

The door of Cabin 28 began to open. Sharp eyes gleamed along the corridor. A black-gloved hand appeared at the edge of the door. Then, the moving figure stopped, while the gleaming eyes remained focused upon the distant bulkhead.

A metal panel was opening slowly outward. The Shadow watched the figure of a man step from the secret cabin. The open panel obscured most of the man's body, and hid his face. His back turned as he closed the panel behind him.

The man was carrying a compact package. He did not turn his face toward the spot where The Shadow stood. Instead, he headed toward the rear of the corridor, only a few yards away, and, with a swift stride, made a dash in that direction.

Scarcely had the man gone before The Shadow emerged from Cabin 28. With gliding motion he set forth in pursuit of the fleeing man.

The destination was obvious. At the rear of the corridor was a stairway that led upward into the envelope above the gondola. There were passages up there, beneath the balloonets; and among those passages The Shadow might trace the course that the man had taken.

It was chance that interfered. Before The Shadow had moved a dozen feet, the door of a cabin farther down the corridor opened, and two officers of the *Munchen* came into view. Coming forward along the narrow way, they would surely have encountered The Shadow, but for the quick action of the black-clad figure.

With a turning sweep, The Shadow regained his cabin. The door closed as the officers tramped by. It reopened, and even while the men were still walking forward in the corridor, The Shadow's amazing form was sweeping toward the companionway at the rear, taking up the delayed pursuit.

A spectral mass of black, The Shadow arrived at the top of the companionway. Straight ahead lay the walk that led to the rear of the dirigible. The interior of the tremendous envelope was a heavy bulk above, with this passage, illuminated only by safety lights, running beneath.

The keen mind of The Shadow was at work. That brain had trained itself to measure time in split seconds to gauge each passing event with absolute precision. The length of the passage within the envelope proved clearly that the man who had emerged from the panel could not have gained its end in the short time allowed him between his departure and The Shadow's swift pursuit.

A tiny light gleamed in a blackened fist. The Shadow was moving along the passage in the envelope, his flashlight pointing out spots on either side. Here were hatchways in the lower surface of the dirigible——places where goods could be taken in or unloaded. The Shadow's light stopped on the hatch nearest to him.

The fastening of this opening was loose. Someone had opened the hinged door and left it loose after it had swung shut. The Shadow's hands opened the light barrier. The blackened head and shoulders thrust themselves through the opening.

The ground was more than a mile below. Tiny glimmering lights indicated the countryside. The flashing of an air beacon showed the airway which the dirigible was following. The Shadow's keen eyes spotted that intermittent signal.

Through those eyes, The Shadow gained a photographic impression of the ground beneath. In daytime, the observation would have been difficult enough; at night, it was far more so. Yet, with the air beacon as his guide, this strange observer was able to gain the exact location of the dirigible. The Shadow was taking the position.

Too late to overtake the man who had fled, The Shadow had gained full knowledge of the man's purpose and action. Somewhere, now miles behind the dirigible, and thousands of feet below, a human form was dropping to safety from the *Munchen,* with the broad surface of a parachute spread out above him!

The Shadow's quarry had made a remarkable and well-planned escape from the moving dirigible. Of passengers and crew, there was only one who had discovered the deed. That one was The Shadow!

No thought of pursuit engaged The Shadow as he made his way back along the passage toward the huge main gondola. There was another task before him. The black-garbed shape flitted down the companionway and entered the corridor of the gondola. It stopped before the secret panel.

Gloved fingers were at work, prying along the narrow crevice that marked the edge of the secret door. It required less than a minute for The Shadow to discover the hidden mechanism. A click resounded as a piece of metal entered the crack. The panel opened, and The Shadow stepped within. The door closed, barely a second before footsteps came down the corridor. The officers were coming back along the passage.

Half an hour passed. The first shafts of dawn, appearing over the horizon, brought a brilliant glint to the silvery surface of the mighty German airship. Those first rays of daylight did not reach the windowless central corridor. That passage was dependent upon the lights that glowed along its low ceiling. They were the lights that showed the panel of the secret room reopening.

The form of The Shadow appeared in the corridor. The panel closed. The spectral shape was ghostly as it made its rapid, silent way to the door of Cabin 28. The door of the cabin opened. The Shadow merged with the gray dawn of the room within.

To-night, within the last hour of darkness, a murderer had left the *Munchen* to gain the safety of the ground below. The dirigible had hours ahead before it reached Chicago. A thousand miles between the Atlantic seaboard and the great metropolis of the Middle West! Somewhere, in that tremendous range, the escaping man had dropped by parachute!

Well could that unknown man suppose that his flight would never be detected. No one could suspect the time and place that he had chosen by random. Yet the fleeing man of crime had not reckoned with The Shadow.

The Shadow knew!

Chapter III

MYSTERY SUPPRESSED

Another night had come. Moored to a gigantic mast at the Chicago airport, the dirigible *Munchen* proudly flaunted itself as the newest conqueror of air and ocean.

The big Zeppelin had been here for hours. Passengers were gone; all formalities were ended. Captain Heinrich von Werndorff, after a tremendous welcome, had returned to his quarters aboard the mighty airship.

A tap at the door. Lieutenant von Salzburg entered. Captain Werndorff greeted him with a care-worn smile. The lieutenant bore a message that was chiefly a reminder.

"Half an hour yet, Herr Captain," he said. "The banquet in your honor——they will be here to take you——"

Von Werndorff nodded. He arose from his desk and gripped the lieutenant's arm.

"Fritz"——Von Werndorff's tone was serious——"the corridor is empty?"

"Yes, Herr Captain."

"Remain here. I shall need you."

The dirigible commander left the cabin and went along the corridor to the secret door in the bulkhead. He tapped softly, using the pick which he had brought from his pocket. There was no response. Von Werndorff smiled. The baron would wait, of course, accepting this tapping merely as a warning of a visit.

Von Werndorff opened the secret panel. He found the room in darkness. Strange, he thought. Could Baron von Tollsburg be sleeping? With impatient alarm, the captain found the switch and illuminated the room.

He stared about him in amazement. The cabin was empty!

The closet door was closed; so was the berth at the side of the room. There was but one inference—that Hugo von Tollsburg had decided to leave the dirigible of his own accord. Yet Von Werndorff could scarcely accept that fact without the formality of an investigation.

He opened the berth, and it dropped down. Like the room, the berth was empty. It would have been quite possible for a man to have been within that berth——to have closed it behind him——to have remained there in hiding. For the berth connected with the ventilator shaft, and thus received air.

Von Werndorff closed the berth. He clicked the catch in the closet door, and opened the barrier.

It was then that Captain von Werndorff stepped back with a gasp of agony. As the little door swung outward, a huddled form toppled with it.

Flattening itself grotesquely on the floor, the dead body of Baron Hugo von Tollsburg came into view! It fell back upward; its livid face and bulging eyes stared, sightless, into the countenance of Captain Heinrich von Werndorff.

Murder!

A fierce cry came from Von Werndorff's throat. Here was the man he respected and obeyed, slain within a secret hiding place, where safety had been guaranteed to him!

For long, miserable minutes, Von Werndorff stared into that dead face. At length the misery of the tragedy dulled. Consternation seized the commander.

A man who gave the utmost attention to detail, Von Werndorff scarcely knew how to act. He had made careful plans for Baron von Tollsburg to leave the airship with the lieutenant; now that these arrangements were rendered useless by the baron's death, the captain was stunned.

Only the growing thirst for vengeance conquered other emotions. Gradually, Von Werndorff found himself reviewing the events that might have brought death to the aristocratic stowaway.

Friedrichshafen. Von Werndorff was sure that no one had followed the baron aboard there. Who knew of the secret compartment aboard the ship? Only the trusted workmen who had aided in its completion, and their knowledge was not complete. Fritz von Salzburg, whom the commander knew could be trusted. Otherwise, only Baron von Tollsburg and Von Werndorff himself.

Unless some one had come aboard beforehand, the entrance to this secret room must have taken place while the dirigible was in flight between Germany and America. Only one man could be suspected. The commander thought of Henry Arnaud.

Why had he not apprehended Arnaud when the man had spoken of stowaways? Von Werndorff cursed his mistake. Yes, it must be Arnaud who had killed.

With a dull feeling of futility, the commander began a hopeless search for evidence. Stooping over the body of his dead friend, he found that Von Tollsburg's pockets had been rifled of all their contents, except a few coins, a pipe and a pouch of tobacco. The killer had been a thief as well as a murderer.

In the berth, Von Werndorff continued his hopeless search. There, however, he discovered two objects; but neither meant anything to his mind. One was the cork-tipped butt of a cigarette; the other was a fragment of torn paper.

The cigarette emanated an Egyptian aroma, and Von Werndorff noted that it bore the name "Pharos." It was evidently an imported brand that was very little known.

The piece of paper carried a scrawled signature——the name of Hugo von Tollsburg, written twice.

Further search revealed nothing.

Von Werndorff folded the cigarette butt within the slip of paper, and placed them in his pocket. He studied the body of the baron with an unhappy gaze, and his mind reverted to the conversation which he had held with Von Tollsburg in this very room.

"No one must ever know——my mission——must be preserved a secret——whatever may occur——not one bit of evidence must remain——"

Whatever the case might be, Von Werndorff could see but one duty; that was to keep the news of this strange death from the world. In forming his decision, the Zeppelin commander was governed by a double motive. First, his promise to the baron; second, his own interests.

It would fare badly with Von Werndorff should the authorities, in either Germany or America, learn that he had intended to land a stowaway in Chicago. An unexplained murder would add to the difficulties of the situation. Silence was paramount. Von Werndorff's duty now lay to himself.

The fact that time was passing became very pressing to the stupefied commander. It forced his immediate decision. He cautiously opened the panel of the cabin, went into the corridor, and reached his own quarters, where he beckoned to Lieutenant von Salzburg. The subordinate followed him back along the long corridor and stood serenely by while Von Werndorff reopened the secret door.

When he entered the room at the commander's bidding, Von Salzburg stood agape at the sight of the murdered man. The young lieutenant did not know Baron von Tollsburg. He had no idea who the dead man might be. He heard the click as the panel closed; then turned to meet his superior's eyes.

"Fritz," said Von Werndorff in a serious tone, "this man was a friend of mine. You brought him aboard the *Munchen;* he remained, and I intended to smuggle him into the United States. He is dead now; and the matter must never be known. You understand?"

The lieutenant nodded.

"It is fortunate," added Von Werndorff, "that our flight was so successful. Within three days we head south for Rio de Janeiro. On our way to Brazil, I shall expect you to perform an important work. Enter this room, place the body of——of my friend in a box, and remove it to the corridor. Be sure that it is weighted after you have taken it up the companionway; then through the hatch——into the ocean——"

"I understand," responded the lieutenant. "I shall assume the responsibility. There are members of the crew whom I can trust. They need never know what the box contains."

"Correct," declared the commander. "You are sure that you can handle this, Fritz?"

"Without difficulty, Herr Captain."

Von Werndorff sighed in relief. He trusted Fritz as he would his own son. By passing the first burden to his subordinate, and letting Von Salzburg employ others to aid him, the commander was clearing the matter to perfection.

Captain Von Werndorff congratulated himself upon his methodical decision as he rode by automobile to the banquet that had been arranged in his honor. Nevertheless, he could not forget the misfortune that had come to his friend, the baron.

Smoldering vengeance still rankled Von Werndorff's thoughts. In his pocket he felt the two shreds of evidence—the cigarette butt and the scrawled signature. He felt sure that Von Tollsburg had smoked the cigarette, and had written upon the paper. Therefore, these articles were no clew to the murderer. They were evidence only that Baron von Tollsburg had been aboard the *Munchen*. Therefore, Von Werndorff did not want them.

As the automobile crossed a bridge, Von Werndorff tossed the folded slip of paper from the window. Weighted by the butt of the cigarette, the tiny object sailed over the rail and dropped into the Chicago River.

Henry Arnaud!

The thought of that man angered Von Werndorff. Fixed in the German commander's mind was the positive belief that Arnaud had been in the secret cabin; that he was responsible for Von Tollsburg's death; that he had overlooked the torn paper and the cigarette stub as articles that were inconsequential. Well did Von Werndorff know that it would be not only futile, but dangerous, to seek Henry Arnaud, now that the man had left the jurisdiction of the dirigible.

In only one chief surmise was Von Werndorff correct; namely, in his suspicion that Henry Arnaud had been in the secret cabin. But Von Werndorff was wrong when he believed that Henry Arnaud overlooked the two fragments of evidence. Arnaud had discovered them; he had left them there; but he had noted them as clews that Von Werndorff had not suspected.

Why would Baron von Tollsburg, whose pipe and pouch showed his preference in tobacco, have smoked a mild Egyptian cigarette? Why, again, would the baron have scrawled his signature twice upon a torn slip of paper?

Von Werndorff had not noted a difference in each signature; nor had he seen the beginning of a third, at the spot where the paper had been torn. Henry Arnaud, alone, had observed these factors.

As The Shadow, he had gained two clews to the murderer; he knew that the man smoked a particular brand of cigarettes—called Pharos—and he knew that the killer had spent his time endeavoring to duplicate the signature of Baron Hugo von Tollsburg.

These objects—like dozens of other cigarette butts and many more slips of scrawled signatures—had evidently been consigned to the ventilator shaft, but had dropped back into the berth.

In his vindictiveness toward Arnaud, Captain von Werndorff shot wide of the truth. Not for one minute did his mind center upon actuality. Little did he know that at that very moment, the man whom he had met as Henry Arnaud was seeking the trail of the murderer who had killed Baron Hugo von Tollsburg!

The Shadow had seen; The Shadow had discovered; The Shadow was bound upon a new mission as an avenger of mysterious crime!

Even while Captain von Werndorff was on his way to the banquet, the work of The Shadow was well under way. The agents of The Shadow had already been ordered on their missions. The Shadow had already started on this trail of murder which might lead to where no one knew—not even The Shadow—as yet!

CHAPTER IV

THE TRAIL

Back along the path which the airship *Munchen* had taken on its trip of death, a lone man watched, parked in his car along a country road. The man was Harry Vincent, agent of The Shadow, and the lowered top of his convertible coupe showed his features as the flashes of an airway beacon streaked the night.

To Harry Vincent, this night was the beginning of a new adventure. Harry's life had been filled with adventures ever since the momentous time when he had met The Shadow. Long ago, a mysterious hand had drawn Harry from the brink of suicide; a whispered voice had bidden him to obey; and henceforth, Harry had served an unknown master.

Stationed in New York, supplied with all the funds that he required, Harry Vincent constantly awaited The Shadow's bidding. A young man of ability and resourcefulness, Harry had proven an excellent operative whenever The Shadow had required him to combat crime.

For the past month, Harry had been free from duty. Then, shortly before noon on this very day, he had received a telephone call from an investment broker named Rutledge Mann. That meant instructions from The Shadow—for Mann was a contact agent, who, like Harry, served The Shadow.

Harry's instructions had been to drive to this lonely spot, and to await certain developments. Harry had arrived two hours ago. He was still waiting in his silent, darkened coupe, the lowered top being also in accord with orders.

A rhythmic hum came from overhead. Harry became immediately attentive. He stared upward and saw a hovering light that twinkled three times.

This was the signal that Harry had expected. He watched the moving light.

The token in the sky was different from that of an ordinary passing plane. It did not move with steady, rapid sweep; instead, it held its position momentarily; then sidled slowly away, twinkling its occasional triplet, like a gigantic firefly seeking for a place to descend.

Harry knew the reason for the odd behavior of the light. This was no ordinary plane above; it was an autogyro, the type of aircraft that The Shadow frequently utilized. At the control of that ship was The Shadow himself. That fact, Harry knew.

The autogyro was picking a circuitous course. Harry started the motor of the coupe. He edged the car into the road and slowly started in the direction which The Shadow's plane had taken.

Now appeared a change in the signal from above. The color of the twinkling light had changed. It was green instead of white. That was the final signal. It meant that the ship was preparing for a descent.

Harry parked the coupe and turned out the headlights. He clambered from his car and ascended a bank beside the road.

The autogyro's lights were hovering with design. Still flashing their green signal, they gave Harry opportunity to head in their direction, and thus note the exact spot of the landing.

Slowly, the machine descended. Above the dim horizon, Harry could see the revolving wing that whirled above the ship. The shape of the autogyro was blotted out as it came to earth close by the trees. Harry was running across the field.

When the young man reached his destination, he saw a tiny glow beside the bulking shape of the autogyro. He knew the meaning of that light. The Shadow had stepped from his plane, and was awaiting the arrival of his agent. Harry stopped a few yards away from the invisible man who held the flashlight. He saw the torch move; and he followed.

What was The Shadow seeking? Why had the mysterious personage of darkness dropped from the night at this isolated spot?

Harry could make no conjecture. Little did he realize that The Shadow was following an air trail; that the autogyro had carefully descended along the course by which an escaping murderer had dropped from the great dirigible *Munchen!*

Silently, Harry followed the man ahead. He could see no outline of The Shadow's form. A larger flashlight was working now, sweeping along the ground as The Shadow led the way in a methodical search.

Suddenly the light stopped. A soft laugh came from above it. Harry shuddered. He had heard that laugh before; it was a laugh which he, as The Shadow's trusted agent, had no cause to fear. Nevertheless, its sinister, whispered tones were uncanny. There was something in that amazing mockery that brought dread to all who heard it.

The laugh of The Shadow!

"Come."

The voice followed the laugh. The single word brought Harry forward. The young man stared at the spot where the flashlight's rays formed a luminous circle upon the ground. There, Harry saw the marks of two feet impressed in the soft earth. The traces of those implanted shoes possessed one noticeable oddity: the left was on the right; the right on the left.

The fact caught Harry Vincent's eye, but his mind gained no explanation. The Shadow's laugh, however, showed that The Shadow understood. A man, descending in a parachute, had landed with crossed legs—in the proper method of terminating a landing via parachute.

These were the marks that The Shadow had come to find; they were the sure trace of the man who had dropped from the swift German dirigible. The Shadow had picked up the trail of the man who murdered Von Tollsburg!

The light moved along the ground; again, Harry followed. Here were faint traces of footprints going toward the clump of trees. Harry himself would have lost the trail; but The Shadow's eagle eye did not fail. With uncanny precision, the bearer of the flashlight followed the course that the murderer had taken.

There was brush among the trees. The flashlight spotted a clump of bushes. A broken branch gave a quick clew. A low command came in The Shadow's whisper. Harry separated the bushes, and there, while the flashlight played ahead, he discovered a mass of crumpled cloth. Dragging out the discovery, Harry spread a parachute upon the ground.

Once again, the keen eyes of The Shadow were taking up the trail along the ground. The path brought the searchers to an embankment. Footprints showed in the earth. They led to the dirt road and mingled with the dust.

Harry Vincent strode along, still behind that light that flickered from an unseen hand. There was something ghostly in the atmosphere. The light itself seemed detached from a human being. Suspended in air, it might have been moving of its own accord, as it searched the dirt of the road and never ceased its progress.

When the light finally stopped, it was at the point where the old road encountered a paved highway. Here, under the scanning glare, Harry could see another telltale mark in a patch of mud. The footprints again, turning down to the left. That was the direction in which the man had gone!

The light went out. Harry Vincent felt a sudden dread amid the gloom.

Out of the darkness came a low, eerie whisper. Its strange note made Harry tense. The Shadow was speaking in a sinister voice that seemed unreal. Only once before had Harry Vincent so fully realized the commanding force of his mysterious master; that had been upon the eventful night when The Shadow had plucked him from death's brink.

"Follow the trail," came The Shadow's words. "The man was here last night. He chose this spot at random—three o'clock—make inquiries—learn his destination—"

The young man understood the vital orders. Some one had dropped from the air. That man had been traced by The Shadow. A stranger in a place chosen through necessity, the man must have sought to gain his location. His first stop would have been a habitation close by.

"I understand," declared Harry.

There was no response from the darkness. Harry hesitated; then realized that he must go back along the road until he reached his car. With the coupe he could take the paved road and run along the trail toward the nearest town. Harry was a trained investigator for The Shadow. He knew how to do the work that was now required of him.

Plodding along the dirt road, Harry experienced the strange sensation that someone was close beside him. The feeling was intermittent; at times, Harry was sure that The Shadow was here; then he would suddenly become convinced that the invisible companion was gone.

When he reached the coupe, Harry clambered into the car and turned on the headlights. The focused glare illuminated the road ahead. Strange, long silhouettes of black spread across the dirt byway. They seemed to sway as Harry watched them; but he could not discern whether any one might be the shadow of a man or merely the blackness caused by some tree beside the road.

The starter clattered; the motor throbbed; and Harry urged the car into gear. As he neared the paved highway, he caught the sound of a purring mechanism. Staring upward, Harry caught a fleeting glimpse of a mass that was lifting itself through the air.

The autogyro! Silently, swiftly, The Shadow had returned to his ship. He was rising now, in his mysterious departure. No lights twinkled. Only the thrum of the motor told of The Shadow's course. The purring died away while Harry Vincent listened from his car.

For Harry Vincent remained with a quest before him. The Shadow, his strange task accomplished, had gone into the upper realm of the night.

While Harry was performing his simple task, The Shadow had more difficult matters to do.

CHAPTER V

IN THE SANCTUM

Another night had come, and with it darkness. But it was not the shroud of night that pervaded this hidden room somewhere in Manhattan. This place was dominated by the blackness of closed walls and ceiling. It was a spot where daylight never came—the sanctum of The Shadow!

Click!

The sharp sound brought light—a strange, eerie glow that filled a corner of the room. A bluish illumination shone upon the surface of a polished table; but the shade above the lamp hid the form that stood close by.

A pair of hands appeared beneath the light. White hands, long hands, they showed sensitive touch combined with latent power. Upon the third finger of the left hand gleamed a shining gem—a radiant stone that glowed with ever-changing hue. From deep maroon, it became mauve; then purple. Its depths sent forth sparkling shafts of light.

This was The Shadow's emblem—the girasol that was his only jewel. A fire opal of rarest luster, this precious trophy was unmatched in all the world. A relic of the Romanoff jewels, The Shadow wore it constantly. With mysterious sparkle, the girasol betokened the strange, unknown personality of the one whose finger it adorned.

When the hands of The Shadow appeared beneath that light, there was work ahead for them. To-night, they were engaged in an important task. They were assembling the shreds of information which The Shadow had gained in his quest to find the murderer of Baron Hugo von Tollsburg.

First the hands produced a report from Harry Vincent. This, by the tabulation which it bore, had come to The Shadow early in the day. The Shadow's girasol sparkled while the left hand held the paper, and the right forefinger pointed to important passages in the report. A low laugh came from the gloom as hidden eyes scanned the lines.

> First logical building from dirt road—service station owned by Asa Rothrock—one mile six-tenths—man stopped there at four o'clock in morning—inquires regarding locality——

The Shadow read on. Harry's report was a mingling of essential and varied facts. It was conclusive in one important point, namely, that The Shadow's agent had unquestionably picked up the trail of the man whom The Shadow sought.

In his investigation, Harry had artfully managed to start Asa Rothrock talking. Two nights ago, the owner of the service station had experienced an interesting episode which he had recounted while Harry had listened in curious interest.

A stranger had knocked at the door of Rothrock's little house. The man had explained that he and a companion had encountered motor trouble with their car. The stranger had decided to let his friend drive on and chance it; but he had thought it best to stop off and seek lodging for the night.

In talking with Asa Rothrock, the man had consulted a road map, and had evidenced surprise to learn that he was only fifteen miles from a town called New Windsor.

Using Rothrock's phone, he had called a garage in that place, and had arranged for a car to come over and pick him up. By taking an early-morning train at New Windsor, the stranger had said that he could make connections for New York.

Rothrock had suggested that the man drive to the town of Dalebury instead, for there he could catch a direct train on another line; but the stranger had preferred New Windsor; and New Windsor it had been.

Harry, after leaving the service station, had gone directly to the garage at New Windsor. There, taking his cue from what Asa Rothrock had told him, Harry had introduced himself as a friend of the man who had used the garage car.

Harry's story had been a good one. He claimed to be the driver of the car that had left the stranger at Rothrock's. He wondered if his friend had decided to stay in New Windsor, or if he had gone on by train. He learned that the stranger had taken an express at six fifteen in the morning.

Neither Asa Rothrock nor the driver of the garage car had given Harry a clear description of the stranger. The man had kept constantly in the darkness, and both were vague when it came to a recollection of facial characteristics. But at the station, inquiring for his pretended friend, Harry had gleaned a piece of information.

The man had put in a telephone call, the telegraph operator had said. It had been a long-distance call to New York, and the man recalled that the stranger had announced himself by giving an odd name over the wire. The operator had not heard the name clearly, and it now escaped her memory.

Since the stranger was supposed to be Harry's friend, it required a bit of bluffing on Harry's part to dodge this dilemma. Harry had managed to do so, stating that since his friend had taken the train, there was no reason for him to wait in New Windsor any longer. The stranger, he learned, had bought no ticket.

* * *

These facts concluded Harry Vincent's report. The Shadow's review was brief. The hands pushed the statement aside and brought out a new sheet.

This had been received by The Shadow within the last hour. It was a brief report from another agent, Cliff Marsland, stating that he had formed new contact with the New York underworld.

The fact that Cliff Marsland was on duty showed that The Shadow had lost no time in following the tip from Harry Vincent, regarding the telephone message to New York.

Cliff Marsland was a valuable operative in the employ of The Shadow. A man with a fictitious reputation as a killer, Cliff had a habit of bobbing up in gangdom at unexpected times.

The denizens of the bad lands looked upon Cliff as a gunman de luxe. In reality, Cliff was serving The Shadow, and his acquaintance with big-shot gang leaders frequently enabled him to handle inside jobs.

The man who had dropped from the German dirigible was a murderer who had come to America. His arrival was unknown to authorities in the United States. The Shadow suspected him as one who plotted further crime. It would be Cliff Marsland's work to watch for any underworld developments that might indicate international activities.

Harry Vincent's report had given definite indications that New York was the goal of the man whom he had trailed. To The Shadow, the obvious was not always the most logical. A low laugh came from the gloom as the white hands spread a large map upon the polished table.

Pointed fingers indicated two spots upon the map. One was the town of New Windsor; the other was the town of Dalebury. Railroad time-tables appeared beside the map. The Shadow was consulting the schedules of through trains.

At Rothrock's the stranger had announced that he was going to New York. Yet—according to both maps and schedules—he had chosen the town that was less suitable. Dalebury was closer to the landing spot than New Windsor. It was a larger place. It afforded a direct line to New York, instead of a connecting one.

Why had the murderer picked New Windsor in preference?

The Shadow knew. Although the man who had fled the airship had made a call to New York, the inference was that he had business elsewhere.

The train that he had taken stopped at a junction point where an hour's wait would bring a New York train; but by remaining on the original train, the man could choose a destination in Connecticut.

The Shadow's fingers indicated two cities. One was New Haven; the other, Hartford.

The fingers remained motionless. Finally, as though guided by deductive thought, the forefinger alone continued pointing. It rested upon the dot that stood for Hartford. There, The Shadow reasoned, was the city which the man had chosen.

Since his arrival in the United States, from the time that he had hurried eastward by air from Chicago, The Shadow had accomplished wonders. His photographic brain; his knowledge of airways; his quick location of position aboard the dirigible—all these had enabled him to drop from the darkness of the sky and find the exact spot where the parachute leaper had landed.

The report from a trusted agent had given The Shadow a clew to the murderer's probable destination. Incredible though it seemed, The Shadow was successfully trailing a man who had gained all the odds. But with all his superhuman accomplishments, The Shadow had not yet gained a knowledge of the murderer's purpose.

The motive which had inspired the man to kill Baron Hugo von Tollsburg was something that The Shadow must discover. If a crime should, at this very moment, be in the making, The Shadow could only hope to solve it after it occurred. Prevention of impending evil would be possible only by closing further on the trail.

Keen intuition was The Shadow's forte. This amazing master of crime detection could scent the approach of impending deeds of evil. The grim laugh that came from the gloom beyond the flickering light of blue gave an inkling of The Shadow's thoughts. The murder of Hugo von Tollsburg could be nothing more than the first step in a chain of contemplated crime.

A man with a mission had been killed. Well did The Shadow know that the death of Hugo von Tollsberg would be suppressed by those who discovered it. Somewhere in the State of Connecticut a fiend of evil was at large, his identity still unrevealed, his purposes as yet unknown.

To-night, The Shadow could do no more than approach the probable scene of the crime, to wait amid the darkness, watching for a stroke that might mean doom. From then on, The Shadow would gain new opportunity.

The rays of blue light disappeared as the switch clicked above the shade. The room was plunged in darkness. Through the silence came the shattering cry of a strange, ghoulish mockery. The walls of the room caught up The Shadow's laugh, and threw it back with impish echoes.

Before the weird reverberations had ended, the sanctum was empty. The Shadow had departed upon a new quest. To-night, he was starting for the vicinity where crime seemed due to strike.

The aftermatch of the sanctum episode occurred on the Boston Post Road later in the evening. A huge, powerful roadster appeared upon that highway, swiftly heading toward the Connecticut border.

The Shadow was on his way to Hartford, the city where he had decided that danger lay!

CHAPTER VI

THE FALSE EMISSARY

The city of Hartford is noted for its exclusive suburbs. Large, spacious mansions, surrounded by ample lawns and secluded by ancient shade trees, are by no means uncommon within the limits of the Connecticut capital.

Such a house was the residence of Winston Collister, a man well known in insurance circles both for his integrity and his wealth. Collister's home was a fine old structure, set far back from the avenue; and its large colonial pillars made it easily recognizable.

The interior of the Collister mansion was magnificent. The rooms were spacious and handsomely furnished. Prompt and efficient servants were on duty. When the Collisters entertained, they did so lavishly; but, as a rule, Winston Collister preferred quiet evenings, and avoided ostentation.

To-night, with midnight close at hand, Winston Collister was seated alone in his library. A tall man of athletic build, the youthfulness of his face belied the age that his gray hair indicated.

Midnight was an unusually late hour for the insurance man. He usually retired before eleven o'clock, except when social affairs were in progress.

Several members of the family had already retired; both of Collister's sons, however, were still downtown. Two of the servants—Ducroe, the butler, and Ogden, the footman—were still on duty. It was Ogden who appeared at the door of the library to inform Winston Collister that a gentleman had called to see him.

"Ah, yes, Ogden," said Collister quietly. Did the gentleman say that he has an appointment with me tonight?"

"He sent in his card, sir."

The millionaire insurance man received the slip of pasteboard. It bore the name:

HUGO VON TOLLSBURG

"I shall see the visitor, Ogden," declared Collister. "Show him into my study. I shall join him there."

The study was some distance from the library; it was a small room located in the wing of the mansion.

Winston Collister stood up after Ogden had gone, and thoughtfully paced back and forth, while he allowed his visitor time to reach the room where the interview was to take place. Then, dignified and erect, the gray-haired man went to meet his guest.

Stepping into the study, Collister faced a man of medium height, whose firm-set face gave him an appearance of importance. The man did not represent the typical German; but his trim, pointed mustache gave him a foreign air. Collister made a detailed study of the man before him.

He was particularly impressed by the visitor's eyes. Dark, steady in gaze, those optics centered themselves upon the millionaire. They were the eyes of a shrewd man; at the same time they possessed an impressive firmness.

"You are Mr. von Tollsburg?" questioned Collister.

"Baron Hugo von Tollsburg, responded the visitor, with a stiff bow. "At your service, Herr Collister."

There was a guttural accent to the speaker's voice, and it offset the slight doubt that Collister had entertained as to the man's actual nationality.

Winston Collister extended his hand. The visitor accepted it, and after the shake, took the chair that the millionaire indicated.

Collister offered cigars. The guest produced a cigarette instead. The millionaire lighted his own perfecto, and sat down. In an indifferent tone, he made a passing remark.

"It is an excellent evening," said Collister.

"An evening which one might long expect," returned the man who called himself Von Tollsburg.

"With the world in turmoil——"

Collister cut off his remark and looked directly at his visitor. The suave-faced man responded with the rest of the sentence:

"—it is our duty to right it."

Winston Collister settled back in his chair as he heard the completion of the sentence. There was no need for further formality. With frankness, Collister spoke to his guest.

"I am glad that you have come," he said. "I have been rather anxious during the last few days. Tell me: have you seen Monsieur Ponjeau lately?"

"Just before my departure from Europe," was the response. "As his special emissary, it was necessary for me to confer with him."

"Of course. You saw him at Lausanne."

"Yes."

"A wonderful man, Ponjeau," spoke Collister, in a low, reflective tone. "When he visited me here, Von Tollsburg, I recognized his sincerity the moment that he began to speak. I am pleased to cooperate in the great work that he has begun. He is a natural leader in international affairs."

"Monsieur Ponjeau is a Frenchman," replied the visitor. "I am a German. Less than fifteen years ago, we were enemies. Now we are friends. We are citizens of the world, Monsieur Ponjeau and I. You are the same, Herr Collister."

The seriousness of the man's tone brought a nod

from the millionaire. Winston Collister arose and faced his visitor with dignity.

"It had been my hope," he declared, "to give my contribution to Monsieur Ponjeau in person. I have long since realized that such would be unwise. I am, therefore, willing to place full trust in an emissary of his choosing. Of course, baron, you have the proper credentials——"

The visitor smiled and bowed. He drew a folded paper from his pocket, and extended it to Collister. The Hartford millionaire examined the document with care. He particularly noted the ornate signature of Aristide Ponjeau, which appeared at the bottom of the sheet. He returned the paper to his visitor and received another document.

This, like the first, also bore the signature of Ponjeau. With it was the written name of Hugo von Tollsburg, the signature scored with needle-pointed impressions, so that it could not possibly be altered.

Collister laid this document upon the table. With no further delay, he went to the wall and slid back a panel which concealed a small, strong safe. Opening the metal door, Winston Collister brought forth a packet.

"Here is the money," he said. "My willing contribution to Aristide Ponjeau's great plan—the World Court of Industry. It is my hope, Von Tollsburg, that the success for which we hope will soon be obtained."

"It is my hope also," responded the visitor.

"I fully appreciate," continued Collister, "that success depends upon proper establishment. Adequately equipped with funds, the World Court can gain recognition from the day of its announcement. Here, baron, is my share—the sum of two million dollars."

Collister opened the packet as he spoke. The action revealed a stack of United States currency—bills of a thousand-dollar denomination. Collister made a gesture toward the heap. The man who called himself Von Tollsburg shook his head.

"A count is not necessary," he said, in a friendly tone. "Your word that all is there will be sufficient for me."

The millionaire bowed and rearranged the packet. He gave it to the visitor, who carefully placed it in his coat pocket. Collister, watching, remarked further.

"I have preserved absolute secrecy," he announced. "No one, besides yourself, baron, knows that I have raised this money and brought it to my home. Monsieur Ponjeau, of course, has received my promise; but you have witnessed its consummation."

The visitor arose and extended his hand. There was the effect of sincerity in his grasp. As the men stepped apart, the visitor turned slowly toward the door. Winston Collister stopped him as though by afterthought, as he saw his guest's hand reaching for the document on the table.

"The signature," stated the millionaire.

"Of course," returned the guest.

The shrewd dark eyes watched Winston Collister draw forth a pen and paper. The objects were laid upon the desk. Collister motioned to a chair. The visitor seated himself and picked up the pen. With sweeping, well-timed stroke, he wrote the signature:

Hugo von Tollsburg

Winston Collister picked up the paper that bore the name. He also examined the document that lay upon the desk, to compare the signatures.

"I shall keep this, baron," he declared, "as your receipt for the money. That, of course, is understood. The main purpose of the signature is to finally establish your identity. I thank you for your courtesy baron——"

Collister's voice broke off. The millionaire was making a closer comparison of the signatures. The visitor watched him, with shrewd eyes gleaming. Standing with hands in his coat pocket, the man who called himself Von Tollsburg clutched the packet of thousand-dollar bills with his left hand, while his right moved significantly in his other pocket.

"Perhaps I am in error, baron," Collister was saying slowly. "Perhaps I am mistaken—but—these signatures do not conform so closely as I had expected."

He glanced up suddenly, and was quick enough to catch the antagonistic gleam in his visitor's eyes. The suave man's expression was changing, but too late. In one brief moment, Winston Collister's suspicions crystallized into firm understanding.

"The signatures"—Collister's voice became frigid—"are enough, Baron von Tollsburg! They tell me that you are not the man to whom I should deliver the money. Your eyes tell me the rest. You are an impostor—a false emissary!"

Collister's hand shot out to grip the visitor's wrist. The man was too quick; he stepped away. With surprising agility, Winston Collister made a lunge toward the false emissary, and with it, the millionaire uttered a loud shout for help.

"Ogden! Ducroe!" was his cry. "Come here at once—to my study!"

The call was loud enough to be heard throughout the house. Collister's quick thrust enabled him to catch the impostor's left arm. The false baron managed to break away and dash to the table, where he seized the paper upon which he had written the forged signature of a dead man. He thrust the paper into his left pocket, with the packet that contained two million dollars of Collister's money.

He swung to meet Collister's next attack, and with the motion he brought his right hand from his pocket. A revolver gleamed in his clenched fist.

* * *

As Winston Collister leaped forward, the door of the study burst open, and two men appeared. They were the servants, Ogden and Ducroe.

Their arrival ended all opportunity for flight without bloodshed. The false Von Tollsburg, who until this moment had sought to make a quick getaway, now acted with furious venom.

His eyes blazed as his finger pressed the trigger of the revolver. A shot burst forth, and Winston Collister's leap came to an end. The millionaire crumpled, a bullet through his heart.

The men at the door did not hesitate. The sight of their master falling dead spurred them to wild effort. They leaped across the room in an attempt to seize the killer.

Had the false Von Tollsburg moved toward them, he would have fallen before the fury of their attack. Instead, however, he drew away; and as he backed across the room, he fired four quick shots.

Two were aimed at Ducroe, and they dropped the man before he had traveled six feet. Ogden was coming on with frenzy, but he, too, was destined to receive the murderer's bullets. The final pair of shots, delivered at close range, brought the footman to the floor.

Three sprawled forms lay as tribute to the killer's fell work. The path to the doorway was open. The false Von Tollsburg did not hesitate to use it. Three times a murderer within the space of a single minute, he made a swift dash toward safety.

Followed by screams that came from women on the second floor, the murderer headed toward the front door. That barrier opened as he neared it, and two young men in dress suits confronted the escaping killer. They were Collister's sons, returned from town at this dramatic moment.

The fleeing man was upon them. He raised his revolver and fired his sixth shot at the first of his antagonists. The other Collister boy struck at the upraised wrist, and in that action saved his brother's life. The aim was diverted, and the bullet lodged in the shoulder of the one toward whom it was delivered, instead of striking him in the heart.

With one foe down, the murderer grappled with the other. The Collister youth was wiry and powerful; for a moment he resisted the killer's attack. Then, the murderer's right hand came free, and he struck with his revolver. The weapon met young Collister's skull, and the youth collapsed.

The delay at the door brought the fleeing man face to face with the most crucial situation he had yet encountered. As he ran down the steps between the huge colonial pillars, the impostor saw that his path was barred by a man in uniform. A patrolman had heard the shots, and was running up the walk with drawn revolver.

Seeing the gleaming revolver in the murderer's hand, the officer stopped short and fired. His first shot was wide; the second also missed its target, although the bullet whistled close by the ear of the approaching killer. There was no response from the murderer's gun; the chambers of the revolver were empty.

The policeman did not realize that fact; and it was his ignorance that made him prey to the murderer's ruse. The third shot from the patrolman's gun would surely have reached its mark; but the officer, seeing the barrel of a revolver thrust directly toward his face, dodged instinctively before firing.

In a trice, the killer was upon him. In their writhing struggle, the gun was wrested from the officer's grasp. A shot resounded, and the policeman fell, slain by a bullet from his own revolver.

The murderer was on his way. Scurrying across the avenue, he gained the lawn beyond, followed by shouts of men who were hastening up the street. People were arriving upon the scene; but the sight of the slain policeman made them hesitate to follow the man who had escaped.

Screams from the Collister mansion told of fiendish work within. The rescuers who had seen the departing murderer preferred the light of the house to the darkness of the lawn on the other side of the avenue.

Smashing his way through all resistance, the impostor had escaped. Only Winston Collister—now dead—could have told the reason for the mad deeds of murder. For the false Baron von Tollsburg, fleeing through the night, had used madness only because method had failed.

In his pocket was the fortune he had come to gain. He had carried away the sum of two million dollars!

CHAPTER VII

THE MYSTERIOUS INVESTIGATOR

Inspector Golshark, of the Hartford police force, was standing in the center of Winston Collister's study. The frown upon his face showed his perplexity. Silent detectives and policemen were gathered about, none offering a suggestion.

"It's a tough case," growled the inspector. "If we had one person who could tell us something, it would be different. But with Collister dead—with the two servants dead——"

The inspector shrugged his shoulders. He glanced at the men about him, muttered something about a flock of dummies, and called police headquarters.

"Nothing doing on the guy that got away?" he questioned. "Yeah, he's had pretty near an hour now. Round up all the suspects you can get. That's the only chance. Plenty of people saw him—no one got a good enough look at him."

A policeman entered the room and spoke to the inspector. Golshark listened. A gentleman had arrived to see Winston Collister. He claimed to be a friend of the dead millionaire.

"Show him in," growled the inspector. "We'll be having a lot like him. Might as well be ready for them."

A few minutes later, a tall, well-dressed man entered the study. Golshark glanced at the arrival, and then stared. The visitor was a man of unusual and distinctive countenance. One could not have told his exact age. Forty years might have been a fair estimate, but a guess would have been speculative. The face that the inspector saw wore a quiet, motionless expression; and its features appeared as though they had been chiseled by a sculptor.

In the light of the study, this man was a being with a human mask. Through that inscrutable countenance gleamed a pair of sharp, brilliant eyes, that faced the inspector unflinchingly. The eyes made Golshark ill at ease.

"Who are you?" demanded the inspector. "A friend of Winston Collister?"

"Yes," returned the visitor, in a quiet, even tone. "My name is Henry Arnaud. I have just driven from New York. I intended to call upon Mr. Collister this evening. I stopped by, even though the hour was late. I have just learned—from the officer at the front door—that tragedy has fallen here."

"Winston Collister has been murdered," declared the inspector. "Two servants and a patrolman killed, also."

Henry Arnaud nodded thoughtfully.

"Are there any clews to the murderer?" he questioned, in his quiet tone.

Inspector Golshark started. Who was this man? Openly declaring himself a friend of the slain millionaire, there was no reason why Henry Arnaud should be denied admittance to Winston Collister's home. But there was something in Arnaud's speech that perplexed the inspector. He sensed that he was dealing with a man of keen intellect—one who seemed coldly capable of conducting his own investigation.

Arnaud's explanation of how he happened to stop here was quite plausible. Inspector Golshark accepted it, but with momentary reservations. The inspector would have been surprised had he known that less than twenty minutes before this man had been at police headquarters.

For Henry Arnaud had learned of Winston Collister's death by the simple procedure of stopping at headquarters to check up on recent local crime.

In the hubbub that had followed the report of the killings at the Collister home, Arnaud had gained the information he wanted without asking a single question. It was that visit that had caused Arnaud to come here—not any acquaintanceship that existed between himself and the murdered millionaire.

"What were the details of Winston Collister's death?" quizzed Arnaud, in a placid tone.

Despite a momentary antagonism, Inspector Golshark found himself describing what had happened—so far as the police had been able to ascertain the facts.

"There was a man in this room," he announced. "Who he was—we don't know as yet. We figure he slipped in here somehow, and Winston Collister found him. People upstairs heard Collister shouting for the servants—Ducroe and Ogden. They came running in.

"The murderer killed the lot—Collister and both the others. Then he hit for the front door. Collister's boys were coming in. He shot down one—young Collister. The other, Jerry, got clubbed with the gun.

"Patrolman Luchner heard the shots out on the avenue. He was running up the walk. The killer got him, too—and then made a getaway across the street. That's the last that was seen of him."

Henry Arnaud nodded.

"Was there any motive for the murders?" he asked.

"None we know of," responded Golshark promptly. "We opened the wall safe—Mrs. Collister gave us the combination—but there's nothing taken from it. Some articles of value there—all untouched. She knew the contents of the safe. We figure that the guy came in here to steal; when he was discovered, he shot his way out. That's all."

Again Arnaud nodded. He looked at the floor and gazed about the room. He asked another question.

"Where are the bodies?"

"Removed," said the inspector. "Collister was here—Ogden here—Ducroe here. We've got that part of it straight. He shot down the old man first, and bumped off the servants when they came in; then ran for it."

"Very unfortunate," mused Arnaud, in a solemn tone. "It is quite a shock to me. I hardly know whether I should go on to Massachusetts or go back to New York. Do you object to my staying here a short while?"

"Stick around," replied the inspector. "Maybe"—he paused to smile—"you may find something we've missed."

"Perhaps," observed Arnaud dryly.

The visitor strolled from the study. Inspector Golshark nudged a detective as a sign for the man to follow. As Arnaud crossed the hall and walked slowly into the library, the sleuth was close beside him. Henry Arnaud sat in a chair; the detective walked across the room and stared through a window.

It was while the man's eyes were away from him that Henry Arnaud spotted a small white object lying on the floor. He dropped his hand and picked up the object. It was a calling card, and Arnaud noted the name it bore as he pocketed the card.

Ten minutes later, Inspector Golshark entered the library to see Henry Arnaud resting with half-closed eyes. The visitor awoke from his doze with a start and smiled wanly.

"I feel better," he remarked. "The long drive—the shock of Collister's death—both were a bit too much for me. I think I shall go back to New York."

"Sorry you won't be able to help us," declared the inspector, with a touch of irony.

"In what way?" asked Arnaud.

"By doing a bit of crime reconstruction," said the inspector. "You seemed so anxious to know the details that I thought maybe you might have spotted a few clews."

A sharp glint came to Henry Arnaud's eyes. His lips compressed. He arose from his chair, and faced the inspector with a challenging gaze. His own voice, though even, carried a stronger touch of sarcasm than had the inspector's.

"I have formed a few assumptions," said Arnaud, "and I presume you might be interested in hearing them. Crime, inspector, is often a matter of detail. I have a peculiar knack for reconstructing scenes, partly through deduction, and partly through intuition. To-night's events, as I visualize them, began in this room."

A puzzled frown came over the inspector's brow. Golshark sensed the challenge in Arnaud's voice. Was the man baiting him, or had this chance visit been made with a purpose?

"Winston Collister," resumed Arnaud, "was reading in this room. He was evidently awaiting a visitor. Otherwise, he might not have been alone here at midnight, with the servants on duty; and, he might have been satisfied with reading one book steadily, instead of choosing different ones and laying them aside."

Golshark followed the direction of Arnaud's gaze. The inspector saw three books lying on the table beside the chair where Arnaud had been sitting.

Arnaud's eyes turned toward the bookcases. Golshark followed again and saw the vacancies from which the books had been removed. Close by were other books, jutting from the rows—but that peculiarity did not exist except at the one spot.

"A trifle impatient," explained Arnaud, "Winston Collister started to take down books, and chose others in their place. The arrival of his guest—announced by one of his servants—caused him to go into the study."

Inspector Golshark was frowning. He saw Arnaud's forefinger point to an ash stand, to the remains of a cigar.

"Collister had been smoking," observed Arnaud. "That is an important point, inspector. Come with me—

perhaps we will find what happened after Winston Collister left this room."

With a gesture to the detective, Golshark followed Arnaud into the study. The other members of the police force had gone. With only the inspector and the detective present, Henry Arnaud resumed his discourse.

"A box of cigars," he commented, pointing to the desk. "Winston Collister offered one to his guest. The man evidently preferred a cigarette—of a distinctive brand, inspector. So Collister lighted a cigar for himself. He smoked it but a short while. Here it is—in the ash stand."

Singularly enough, Inspector Golshark was fuming at his own stupidity. He had been sure that Collister had surprised an intruder, and he had overlooked this point that should have been so obvious.

"Examination will show the cigar to be of the same brand as the one in the library," continued Arnaud. "You can make that inspection later on. What concerns us now is the conversation that must have passed between Collister and his guest.

"The fact that Collister quietly laid his cigar aside indicates that he performed some action before he was attacked. I am sorry that you opened the wall safe, inspector. Otherwise, I might be able to prove that Collister took something from it.

"That is purely speculation. What I do know is that Collister laid an object upon this desk—in fact, not only an object, but some papers."

Golshark recalled that he had seen Arnaud look at the desk, when he was in this room before. Now he stared in wonder as the impromptu investigator indicated certain marks that had escaped his notice.

"Just a trifle dusty," observed Arnaud, pointing to the desk. "Enough so that an object placed there—perhaps a package—would leave its trace. Note the smudges of fingers that picked the object up. Two hands, sliding, several inches apart."

Inspector Golshark stared in amazement, and the detective followed his example. Henry Arnaud quietly pointed to another spot, and there showed a very slight impression with an extended smudge beneath it. He pointed out a recurrence of this phenomenon at a portion of the desk where a chair stood.

"A document of some sort," commented Arnaud. "A document, laid here. Let us suppose, inspector, that the visitor showed some credentials to Winston Collister; that in return, Collister gave the visitor a package; and then requested a receipt.

"This pad"—Arnaud paused as he pointed to an innocent-looking object at the side of the desk—"is a new one. One sheet has been torn from it, as you can see by simple examination. Pen and ink—our unknown visitor signing—and then—"

"Then what?" demanded Golshark, in spite of himself.

"Then the trouble," asserted Arnaud. "A signature that did not satisfy. The visitor had received what he desired. Collister wanted it back. The result—murder. The killer went away with the credentials, signature, and stolen goods."

"Yeah? Wait a minute." Golshark had reached the limit of his patience. "Go back a bit. You said something about a cigarette. I suppose the guy that got away was smoking one, eh?"

"He smoked one."

"Say—you seem to think you know a lot about this——"

"I know the ways of certain criminals."

"Yeah? Maybe you know who this one was?"

"No. I might tell you the name which the man assumed. I might tell you of a murder that he performed before. But I cannot—as yet—reveal his true identity; nor do I know what he came here to obtain."

"If you think you're pulling a fast one," came Golshark's antagonistic growl, "it's time you got the idea out of your noodle. This boloney about a guy smoking a cigarette—"

Henry Arnaud raised his hand. Inspector Golshark glowered and became silent. There was something in Arnaud's action that showed he intended to put his theory to the proof.

Carefully, Arnaud lifted the cigar from the ash stand and laid it on the desk. He pointed to the partly consumed end.

"That cigar," he declared, "was smoked longer than the time it takes to smoke a cigarette. Here, in the vortex of the ash stand, we see traces of light ash that indicate a cigarette. The smoker finished his cigarette. Naturally, when a hollow-legged ash stand is available, one drops his cigarette into it.

"Let us hope, inspector, that this ash stand was emptied recently. If so, we will find but one cigarette within it—a cigarette of a very peculiar brand—a cigarette which bears the name 'Pharos' upon its cork-tipped stump. Remember that name. 'Pharos.' "

As he spoke, Henry Arnaud seized the ash stand and swung it high above the desk. He inverted it, and a tiny white object fell out.

As Arnaud thumped the ash stand back to the floor, the inspector leaped forward and seized the object that had dropped. It was the cork-tipped remainder of a cigarette.

With the detective staring over his shoulder, Golshark eyed the stump. Upon it he read the name of the brand —the single word:

Pharos

Inspector Golshark was stupefied. His lips were moving as he mumbled words of amazement. Three full seconds ticked by as Golshark dully realized that this remarkable discovery substantiated all the other statements that Henry Arnaud had made.

With a sharp grunt, Golshark threw the cigarette butt on the desk and shoved the detective to one side as he turned to challenge Henry Arnaud.

"Hey, you——"

The words stopped short. Inspector Golshark blinked in rage. The man that he wanted was no longer here! When he had set the ash stand back upon the floor, Henry Arnaud had walked from the room, while Golshark and the detective were pouncing upon the cigarette butt.

"Get that guy!" cried Golshark, thumping the detective. "Get him—he knows too much——"

The inspector was springing from the room, with the detective at his heels. His shouts, as they reached the hall, brought a policeman running from the front door.

"Where is he?" demanded Golshark. "Arnaud—the wise-faced guy——"

"He went outside, inspector.

"Get him! He may be the bird we want—the murder, come back. Hurry!"

Golshark was springing forward like an enraged bull. As he reached the front door, he caught a fleeting glimpse of a tall form at the sidewalk of the avenue. Drawing a revolver, the inspector shouted a command to stop.

"Hey! Arnaud! We want you!"

A taunting laugh rippled from the darkness. Its eerie tones made Golshark falter. Then, with an oath, the inspector raised his revolver and fired at the spot where the man had been.

Another burst of mockery was the reply. Golshark dashed forward as he heard the gibe.

"Get him! Get him! Spread out!"

Other police were coming in answer to Golshark's order. They scurried in various directions, hoping to discover the man who had so quickly disappeared. Golshark, uttering wild imprecations, stood alone at the end of the walk.

A car swirled along the avenue. Only its dash lights were illuminated. Golshark looked after it as it went by, and noted that the tail light was out. He could not see the license tag.

To Golshark, the car meant nothing, until he heard the strident cry that came from its interior.

The laugh again! Long, loud, and creepy, it burst through the night with sinister merriment. Curses died on the foiled inspector's lips. He saw the car swing up a side street, and in an instant it was blotted out by darkness. The echoes of the laugh still persisted.

The laugh of The Shadow! Though Inspector Golshark had never heard it before, he recognized it as the token of some amazing personage, and in his heart he knew that the man who had sent that laugh was too clever to be apprehended now.

The mysterious investigator was gone. As Henry Arnaud, he had come; as The Shadow, he had departed. Too late to find the spot where the murderer had been destined to strike, The Shadow had gained new clews.

He had seen the traces of crime an hour after it had taken place. He was closing on the trail of the supercrook who used murder as a stepping stone to wealth.

This was barely the beginning of crime. The Shadow knew that murder would strike elsewhere. But until he had gained closer access to the unknown killer, The Shadow could only follow the murderer's trail.

It was not the way of The Shadow to await the acts of criminals. Before the murderer struck again, the master mind would find some method of thwarting the killer's purpose. Already, in New York, The Shadow had placed a trusted agent on an important task .

By to-morrow night, if The Shadow's calculations were correct, a link would be gained between evil doers in Manhattan and the daring slayer who had brought death to Hartford.

The Shadow's course was directed to New York. There he might find the answer that he sought.

CHAPTER VIII

IN THE UNDERWORLD

In Hartford, crime had struck. In New York, crime was brewing. Twenty-four hours after the bold murders had occurred in the capital of Connecticut, Cliff Marsland could scent the impending signs of contemplated crime within the confines of Manhattan.

Cliff Marsland held an enviable reputation in the underworld of New York. He had done time in the big house, otherwise known as Sing Sing. Since his discharge from prison, he had been prosperous, without molestation by the police. That classed him as an ace in the bad lands. Whenever Cliff Marsland appeared in the underworld, he carried a bankroll that would choke a giraffe.

With no gang affiliations, Cliff rated as a free lance among gunmen, and never suffered observation from the authorities. He was in a class by himself. His reliability was an axiom; but his activities were unknown.

Men of the underworld did not realize that Cliff Marsland had gone to prison for a crime that he did not commit; that he had taken the rap to keep stigma from the brother of the girl whom he loved.

Only The Shadow knew that fact; because of it, The Shadow had enlisted Marsland in his service. Cliff was a trump card in The Shadow's hand. The Shadow was using him now.

When Cliff returned to the realm of the underworld, after a period of absence, he immediately frequented the places where gangsters of consequence could be found.

They welcomed him and talked with him. His poker face encouraged information. Cliff Marsland could learn plenty on short notice. He was doing so at present.

Cliff was at the Palace Havana, a night club where flashy mobsmen appeared with their molls. He was working under orders from The Shadow, looking for contacts that would bring him in touch with secret crime of great proportions.

One by one, Cliff had chatted with old acquaintances. Here, in a secluded corner, away from the crowded dance floor, he was hearing news from a shrewd-faced gunman known as "Skeeter" Wolfe.

"Sittin' pretty, eh, Cliff?" Skeeter was saying. "Well, things ain't so bad with me, boy. Not so bad!"

"You know me, Skeeter," responded Cliff. "I'm always in on the mazuma, but I never pass up a good lay. I take the gray while it's hot—and I keep it."

"Big stuff, Cliff?"

Cliff Marsland shrugged his powerful shoulders. A slight smile appeared upon his firm, straight lips.

"It's the way I handle things, Skeeter," he said sagely. "I figure that if a big shot wants four men to do a job, he'll listen to reason when he finds one who will do the work of four.

"It's better for him; it's more dough for the fellow that does the heavy work. That's how I make out. One keeps mum where four don't. Get me?"

"I keep mum, Cliff."

"Sure you do, Skeeter. You're working on something now. Keep it to yourself. You're getting paid for it."

"How do you know?" queried Skeeter, in astonishment.

"Skeeter," laughed Cliff, "if the guy you're working for wants another rod on his payroll, tell him to see me. Tell him I not only keep mum; but I don't give a tip-off."

"How do you mean?"

"I don't show that I'm sitting pretty. You wouldn't know it if you saw me when I was pulling something big. But I can tell by looking at you that you're on a lay."

"You've doped it right, Cliff."

There was admiration in Skeeter's tone. The gangster seemed to be asking for advice; and Cliff furnished it.

"You come here when you're flush, don't you?" quizzed Cliff. "You stay away when things are going slow? Am I right? Well, that's a give-away. I'm the opposite. When I'm sitting pretty, I lay low. When things aren't so good, I blossom out."

"Say, Cliff, that's a good racket. Ain't things so hot with you right now?"

"I've got jack," responded Cliff, in a noncommittal tone. "But I wouldn't mind digging up some more. I'm ripe for it right now. That's why I said to tell your boss that he can get me if he needs me."

"I'm tellin' him, Cliff, to-night. You're a great guy. So is the bird I'm workin' for. I don't mind lettin' you know who he is. Bumps Jaffrey."

Cliff nodded as though the matter did not interest him. Skeeter Wolfe accepted this as cause for further palaver. Comment on Cliff's part might have stopped Skeeter's flow of guarded information; but since Cliff did not appear particularly impressed, Skeeter was anxious to cut a figure.

"It ain't no ordinary job," he said. "It's somethin' big, Cliff. Bart Shallock is in on it. He's a slick guy. I don't even know what it's all about, but when Bart Shallock hooks up with Bumps Jaffrey, it means somethin' is doin'."

"Bumps Jaffrey was a gang leader of repute—one who assembled capable gorillas, and threw them into mercenary service for big shots who required aid. Bart Shallock was a smooth confidence man who consorted with jewel smugglers, blackmailers, and workers of international caliber.

For two nights, Cliff had been thinking about Bart Shallock, along with others. This information was of the type he wanted to gain.

When Bart Shallock required the services of a gang leader, it meant that big matters were at stake. It indicated strong-arm tactics and probable murder as a necessary requisite to a smooth and crafty plan. Here was the very lead that Cliff needed, and he wanted to know more from Skeeter Wolfe.

"Keep mum, Skeeter," warned Cliff. "Don't bother to speak to Bumps Jaffrey. I know him. I'll run into him, and let him know I'm looking for a hook-up. What you know means something while you know it. Don't let other people in on it."

"Sure thing, Cliff," agreed Skeeter. "You're right. Don't think I'd spill the chatter to everybody, though. You're about the only guy I'd talk to."

Uppermost in Cliff's mind was the desire to encounter Bumps Jaffrey; but he gave Skeeter no inkling that the matter was of great importance. Instead, Cliff feigned indifference, and made no effort to break away from Skeeter's company.

It was not long before Skeeter tired of the atmosphere at the Palace Havana, and grunted a good night as he left the place. Cliff waited.

Unless Bumps Jaffrey were coming here, the logical place to find him would be at Brindle's restaurant on Broadway. Cliff left the night club, and started for the eating house. He reached his destination, and entered the popular restaurant.

Brindle's was a paradoxical place. It attracted persons of many classes: theatrical stars, hotel dwellers, chance passers, and gunmen. The place was completely devoid of gawking sightseers.

Radio celebrities passed unnoticed: well-known politicians were unrecognized. So it was with gangsters. Few, except their companions, knew their identity.

Cliff Marsland, when he entered, might well have been a football coach from some mid-Western college. His athletic build gave him that appearance, and his chance arrival marked him as one who had stopped in Brindle's for the first time.

But Cliff was alert as he made his way to the rear of the cafe. There were open tables in the center, but on either side were boxlike booths that regular customers preferred.

From the corner of his eye, Cliff spotted two men in a booth talking over their coffee and sandwiches. One of these was Bumps Jaffrey. Cliff did not recognize the other.

Raising his eyebrows as a sign of recognition, Cliff stopped by the booth, and nodded to Bumps. The gang leader motioned to him to sit down. He introduced Cliff to his companion, who proved to be an acquaintance not concerned with the underworld. Cliff gave an order, and was still eating when the others finished. The odd man left, and Cliff was alone with Bumps.

"How're things going?" questioned Bumps.

"So-so," responded Cliff, indifferently. "Just came back to the big burg. Glad to be here again."

"What're you doing now?"

"Nothing. I don't fool with small stuff, Bumps."

"I know that, Cliff. Maybe you try to hit too big, though."

"Not me, Bumps. I like jobs that are different. Anybody can hire dumb gorillas. I take work that needs brains. I want my share, but I'm not exorbitant."

The final word pleased Bumps Jaffrey. Cliff Marsland had the appearance and manner of a gentleman; but his strong face and powerful physique fitted in with the required standards that the gang leader desired.

"I may need you later on, Cliff," suggested Bumps, in a casual tone. "Where will you be keeping yourself?"

Cliff shrugged his shoulders; then, in a noncommittal tone, he responded that he was frequently at the Palace Havana, and also at Brindle's.

"I'll see you later, Cliff," nodded Bumps, glancing at his watch. "I've got a few gats working for me right now. I may need a real good one soon. Remember, I'm keeping you in mind."

Cliff saw what Bumps was trying to conceal. It was a sure bet that Bumps already had some work under way—a substantiation of what Skeeter had said to-night.

The fact, as Cliff sized it, was probably that Bumps had too many gangsters rather than too few. It would be good policy to meet Bumps right along. Gang depletions were by no means uncommon in New York. Cliff figured himself next in line when a vacancy might come.

That, however, did not solve to-night's problem. Bumps Jaffrey was going somewhere. Despite his feigned manner of leisurely departure, it was probable that he had an important appointment.

Could it be with Bart Shallock?

Cliff decided that it might be.

There were two reasons why Cliff now faced an emergency. His forte was strong-arm work, not ability in following a trail. Furthermore, he could not afford to run the risk of incurring suspicion if he intended to deal with Bumps Jaffrey later on. Nevertheless, Cliff was determined to follow the gang leader.

When Bumps Jaffrey had sauntered from Brindle's, Cliff restrained himself for a few minutes; then took up the trail in hope that he might have luck. Fortune smiled. On Broadway, Cliff saw Bumps hailing a taxicab at the corner below. Hurriedly, Cliff entered another cab, and ordered the driver to follow the one ahead. The taximan obeyed.

Bumps was headed for a location on the East Side. Cliff, cautioning his own driver with a low growl, kept well in the rear. When he saw the front cab pull up at the curb, he ordered his own man to stop.

On the sidewalk, Cliff saw Bumps enter an alleyway.

Walking past the entrance to the alley, Cliff saw that it formed a street with no outlet. He kept on, and reached a corner cigar store. There, he went into a telephone booth, and called a number. A quiet voice responded:

"Burbank speaking."

The tones of that voice eased Cliff's anxious mind. Burbank was a man whom he had never seen. An invisible agent of The Shadow, this quiet-voiced individual was constantly on duty as contact man between The Shadow and his active agents.

Cliff Marsland, like Harry Vincent, made emergency reports through Burbank. Each agent knew the particular phone number where Burbank was located. Calls always brought an immediate response. Messages were promptly relayed to The Shadow.

To-night, as Cliff tensely explained the situation, he received word from Burbank to put in another call within fifteen minutes.

Cliff gave the location of the alley where he had last seen Bumps Jaffrey. After he hung up the receiver, he loitered about the store until the allotted time had ended.

His second call to Burbank brought another prompt response. This time Cliff Marsland received instructions.

"Off duty," were Burbank's words. "Report to-morrow morning to our man."

"Our man" meant R. Mann—Rutledge Mann, whose investment office was a place where The Shadow's agents went to gain instructions, and to deliver their reports.

Cliff Marsland smiled to himself as he rode northward in a taxicab, bound for the Palace Havana. A few more hours at the night club might be useful; but in the back of his head, Cliff felt an assurance that he had accomplished his real work to-night.

Crime was brewing in the underworld. Bumps Jaffrey had assembled a mob. To-night, Bumps Jaffrey was conferring with some one. What might be happening at the conference was something that Cliff Marsland could not conjecture. But he felt confident that it would not remain a secret.

For Cliff had tipped off The Shadow. Even now, the mysterious personage of darkness might well be on his way to look in upon the affairs of Bumps Jaffrey!

CHAPTER IX

THE MEETING

The alley which Bumps Jaffrey had entered was a dismal thoroughfare that gained its dim light from the grimy windows of old houses at the sides.

It was into one of these buildings that Bumps had gone; and now, half an hour after he had left Brindle's restaurant, the gang leader was seated at a table in the corner of a large, dingy room.

The place was a speakeasy known to its patrons as Duke's. This was in deference to the proprietor, a big, wide-faced fellow whose grinning mouth displayed a glittering array of gold teeth, and who had gained the sobriquet of "Duke."

Away from the usual haunts of gangsters, Duke's place was frequented only by those mobsmen who were well known to the proprietor. Hence the speakeasy was not familiar to Cliff Marsland; and it also afforded an excellent spot for Bumps Jaffrey to meet a friend unobserved.

Duke, the proprietor, was a cagy individual. He knew the manner in which mobsmen were wont to frequent a place in ever increasing numbers, until it became nothing more than a hangout for gangs, and forced the proprietor to obey the dictates of outsiders.

This was a condition that Duke did not want, because his speakeasy was doing business as neutral territory. Hence, Duke was very tactful in his methods. He had gained the services of a handful of indiscriminate rowdies who imbibed free drinks, and were always ready to eject any undesirables.

If unwanted mobsters entered Duke's place, the strong-arm squad handled them tactfully, especially if they knew the visitors to be tough. It was easy enough to approach a gangster, and to suggest going to a place where drinks were better.

But when an unknown stranger came in, he was merely ordered to scram; and if he failed to do so, a swift bounce invariably followed.

Bumps Jaffrey, hard-faced and shrewd of eye, liked Duke's place, because of the protection it afforded; and to-night, he had chosen it as a spot for a rendezvous. Imbibing a drink, he watched the door of the speakeasy, and his eye lighted as he saw a newcomer enter.

This man had none of the marks of the underworld. He was above medium height, well dressed, sallow in complexion. His face was intelligent and placid. He bore himself like a gentleman. There was quiet ease in his manner, and he rendered himself quite inconspicuous as he took a table.

After one drink, the stranger quietly arose and walked through a door at the rear of the room. Only two persons saw him go in that direction. One was Bumps Jaffrey; the other was Duke, the proprietor.

Both knew the identity of the stranger. He was Bart Shallock, one of the smoothest confidence men in New York, a clever crook whose activities were the despair of international detectives.

It was with Bart Shallock that Bumps Jaffrey had the appointment.

A few minutes after the confidence man had gone through the door, Bumps quietly arose and went in that direction. At the same moment, the door of the speakeasy opened, and a sweater-clad gangster came into the place.

This newcomer saw Bumps Jaffrey going into the back room. He also observed Duke's watchful eye following the gang leader.

The sweatered man sidled into a chair at a corner table. It was there that Duke spied him. The proprietor came across the room with a challenging air.

"Hey, you!" he demanded. "What're you doin' in here? Why'd you come to this place?"

"This is a speak, ain't it?" came the response, in a gruff tone.

"Sure it is," admitted Duke, with a sour-grinned flash of his gold molars. "But it ain't open to the public."

"I ain't the public," growled the newcomer. "Get me a drink an' make it snappy!"

Duke's big paw shot out and gripped the gangster's sweatered shoulder. With a powerful heave, Duke yanked the man to his feet. He intended to throw the intruder into the alley; and as a preliminary action, he shot a swift punch with his free hand.

The blow never landed. From his crouching position, the sweatered gangster straightened and tilted his head away from Duke's sweeping fist. The proprietor missed his punch, and the gangster countered with a short uppercut that landed on Duke's jaw. Down went the big man, his gold teeth flashing from his wide-open mouth.

Duke, the tough speakeasy proprietor, had been flattened with a single punch. It brought a gasp of surprise from the rowdies about the room. Then, with one accord, five men leaped forward to seize the sweatered gangster.

The first man's head shot up as a tight fist clipped his chin. The others leaped upon the amazing fighter in hopes of bearing him to the floor. He wrested away, and sprang across the room.

They were after him again; and revolvers gleamed as the strong-arm squad came into new action. With two men down, they were taking no chances.

Their adversary was too quick for them. Seizing a chair, he swung it against the nearest man, just as the ruffian aimed his gun. Down went the armed bouncer. The man in the sweater swung the chair high above his head, and as the attackers ducked, he smashed one of the two large lights that illuminated the room.

Turning, he used the chair to whack the arm of another man who was ready with a gun; and before the others could bring weapons into play, he hurled the chair with terrific force toward the second light that hung from the ceiling. A pop and the sound of glass clattering in the darkness. Then the spats of flame from revolvers as the strong-arm men fired at the spot where their adversary had been.

The front door banged, and in response the men surged in that direction, confident that the sweatered man had fled. Two of them reached the alley, but they could see no sign of the man they wanted. When they came back, they found a candle burning. Duke was groggily inserting a bulb in one of the light sockets.

"Did you get him, boys?" questioned the proprietor.

"Naw," responded one of the bouncers. "He scrammed. We was too late to nab him."

"Yeah? Well, it was bum stuff usin' them rods. The coppers might come in on us. I told youse guys always to lay off the shootin'."

Duke finished his task with the bulb, and went to the second socket. When the speakeasy was again thoroughly illuminated, the proprietor went to the back room and ascended a flight of stairs. He stopped at a door on the second floor, and knocked. An anxious voice came from within:

"That you, Duke?"

"Yeah."

"What was the fireworks?"

"We had to get rid of a tough guy, Bumps. He's gone now. Scrammed when it got too hot for him."

"All O.K. now?"

"Looks that way, Bumps. Not enough trouble to bring the coppers."

"O.K., Duke."

Duke went downstairs, growling to himself. He was sorry that the intruder had escaped. A killing meant nothing to Duke, and since gunplay had taken place in his speakeasy, he would have preferred a dead body to an escaped trouble-maker. However, all was quiet, and Duke gave no more thought to matters upstairs.

Had Duke remained in that upper hall, he would have witnessed a surprising sight. A huddled figure emerged from the darkness. The sweatered gangster stood before the door where Duke had been.

The man had not gone out by the front door; instead, he had deceived his enemies in the dark. He had slammed the front door, and had doubled back upstairs.

Standing in the dim light of the hall, the unknown gangster began a strange transformation. He raised the bottom of his sweater, and drew forth a folded mass of black cloth. As the huddled figure drew itself erect, the cloth became a cloak, which drooped over the gangster's shoulders.

A flattened object appeared, and was molded into a slouch hat, which went upon the figure's head. Black gloves slipped over white fingers.

The sweatered gangster had become The Shadow!

A low, whispered laugh shuddered from unseen lips. Stooping, the spectral form leaned close to the door of the room where Bumps Jaffrey was conferring with Bart Shallock. The buzz of voices was scarcely audible. With black-gloved fist, The Shadow knocked at the door.

"Who's there?"

It was the questioning voice of Bumps Jaffrey.

"Duke," came the response from the being in black. The voice was a perfect replica of Duke's growl.

"What's up?" questioned Bumps, from within the room.

"Nothin' "—it was Duke's voice again—"but I'm just playin' safe. Goin' to switch out the light, here in the hall. So you won't be bothered."

"O.K., Duke."

Out went the light. Silence reigned in the hall. Then, slowly and noiselessly, the door of the room began to open. Unseen and unheard, the tall figure of The Shadow moved through the space!

By turning out the light in the hall, The Shadow had prevented any glow from that direction. Now he was entering a dimly lighted room where Bumps Jaffrey and Bart Shallock were seated at a table in the corner.

Both were engaged in conversation; the single light extended from the wall beside their table. Neither glanced in the direction of the door. Hence they did not see the spectral form as it made its arrival.

The Shadow did not linger. The door closed behind him. His tall shape moved across the room like an apparition. He reached a spot where a second table was located, and there merged with the darkness of the wall. Completely invisible, The Shadow listened to the words that passed between gang leader and confidence man.

"I'm not kicking," Bumps was saying. "I'm just wondering, that's all, Bart. I've got the gang watching this guy Venturi, but he's sitting still at the Dexter Hotel, and there's nothing doing. I thought we were set for action."

"Plans were changed for the first job, Bumps," replied Bart Shallock, in a suave voice. "You'll be in on the second."

"You mean the first job has been pulled?"

"Yes."

"Who did it?"

"Crix swung it himself."

Bumps Jaffrey whistled.

"Say, Bart," was his comment, "this bozo Crix must be an ace. I can't figure him."

"You're not supposed to figure him, Bumps. I don't even know who he is myself."

"You've seen him, though."

"Of course. But Crix is the only name he gave me."

"This lay bothers me, Bart," said Bumps, in an uneasy tone. "I don't quite get it. If Crix was after Venturi, why didn't he get Venturi?"

"Bumps," returned Bart, "I don't know the details myself; but I'm going to tell you all I do know. Crix said it would be all right. He will need you shortly, and he knows that you are capable. So I'm going to explain all that's necessary."

"Shoot."

"Well," continued Shallock, "this fellow Crix dropped in to see me more than a month ago. He had me guessing from the minute he began to talk. He knew plenty about me—enough to make a lot of trouble; and when it developed that he was offering me a proposition, I listened.

"He asked me if I had ever heard of Victor Venturi. Of course, I said I had. Crix told me that he had been to Europe, and that he had learned Venturi was tied up with some big proposition. That sounded logical; Venturi used to be a pretty important man in Italian politics. An undercover agent—now retired.

"Crix said that Venturi would come to America on secret business—something involving plenty of money—and that by covering Venturi, we could come in on the dough. Crix wanted me to have a mob ready, and to keep some one like you watching Venturi. That's how it started.

"But after that, Crix discovered something new. Venturi is here on business, yes—but Venturi is the blind. The real negotiations for money were turned over to another man!"

"Then we've got on the trail of the wrong guy!" exclaimed Bumps Jaffrey, in a disgusted tone.

"Yes"—Bart Shallock weighed his answer—"and no. Crix has found the right man. He is handling the job. But if Venturi finds out that matters are going sour, he will step in and make trouble. Venturi is the safety man, Bumps. It's our job to eliminate him so that Crix can do his work."

"That's different."

"Crix came in to see me to-day," continued Bart. "He ran into trouble on the first job. He made a getaway, but it was close. He doesn't intend to take chances. He wants Venturi covered; he wants men ready to help him on the next job."

"I get you, Bart."

"So it's up to you to be ready, Bumps. Keep covering Venturi. Keep watching anyone who is interested in what he does. Be ready for quick orders."

"Right."

Bart Shallock drew a roll of bills from his pocket. He counted off some notes of large denomination.

"Ten grand, Bumps," said the confidence man. "That's just the beginning. Satisfied?"

"You bet!" exclaimed Bumps Jaffrey.

Bart Shallock arose. Without further word, he walked from the room.

A few minutes later, Bumps Jaffrey followed. Confidence man and gang leader had completed their conference.

Blackness stirred on the other side of the room. The figure of The Shadow came into view. Tall, spectral, like a living ghost, the mysterious form of darkness stood in the center of the deserted room. The low, whispered laugh of The Shadow raised sinister echoes.

The black-garbed phantom followed the path that the others had taken. At the bottom of the stairs, a gloved hand turned the knob of the door that led into the speakeasy. There were only two men there now—Duke and another. They were engaged in conversation.

Unobserved, The Shadow stepped into the big room. Gliding along the wall, his figure moved like a living silhouette until it reached the outer door, where it mysteriously disappeared. Neither Duke nor the other man caught a glimpse of the weird form.

A soft laugh reverberated through the alleyway. Then The Shadow was lost in the darkness. To-night, The Shadow had learned the name by which the supercrook was known—the odd name which Harry Vincent had learned about, but had not heard.

Crix! That was the sobriquet of the man The Shadow wanted—the stranger who had dropped from the dirigible *Munchen*. His real identity was unknown even to Bart Shallock, his chief lieutenant.

The Shadow was dealing with a supercrook—a man whose ways were mysterious, whose very person was obscure. The Shadow had not learned where Crix might be; but he had learned the name of the man Crix had ordered watched.

Victor Venturi—one time secret agent for the Italian government—now here in New York at the Dexter Hotel. That was all the clew The Shadow needed. Crix was watching Venturi. The Shadow would watch Venturi also.

Two hunters after the same quarry; but one hunter would be watching for the other. Through their mutual interest in the affairs of Victor Venturi, a meeting between Crix and The Shadow would be inevitable. And the Dexter Hotel would be the scene. That fact, The Shadow knew.

The Shadow always knows!

CHAPTER X

WORD FROM ABROAD

A tall man entered the lobby of the Dexter Hotel, carrying a suitcase. A bell boy relieved him of his burden, and the man approached the desk. He signed the name Henry Arnaud to the register.

While the clerk was reading the signature, this new guest spoke in a quiet, even voice:

"I would like a room on the eleventh floor; one that opens on the west side of the courtyard."

The clerk looked up in surprise. This was an unusual request. He fancied that the guest had been here before, and had been satisfied with a room in that portion of the hotel.

"Very well, Mr. Arnaud," he said. "I shall give you Room 1108."

A man standing near the desk watched Henry Arnaud go to the elevator. This observer then strolled across the lobby and approached a man who was seated at a writing desk.

"Say, Jerry," he said, "I just spotted a guy that we'd better watch."

"Yeah? Why?"

"He picked a room on the eleventh floor. Inside room. Maybe he wants to keep an eye on Venturi."

The other man nodded. The pair were gangsters, in the employ of Bumps Jaffrey. Their faces gave an inkling of the trade which they followed, but at the Dexter Hotel, which had reached a decadent stage, the management was not particular about the social characteristics of the guests.

A few minutes later, the two gangsters went up in the elevator. They found the location of Room 1108, and watched the door for a short while. When they went away, it was because they were convinced that Henry Arnaud had retired. From now on, the new guest would be under surveillance of Bumps Jaffrey's men.

Within his darkened room, Henry Arnaud was smoking a cigar beside the open window. He had closed the transom above the door, but had left a small crack open. This had deceived the gangsters. They had fancied that they could not be heard in the outside hall; but they were wrong. Arnaud's keen ears had heard them arrive; Arnaud also heard the mobsmen leave.

The new guest laughed softly as he opened his suitcase, which lay upon the bed. In the darkened room, he began a transformation. Within a few minutes, the room seemed devoid of any person, yet a living presence still remained. Henry Arnaud had become The Shadow!

A figure slowly thrust itself through the open window. Head and shoulders; then body and legs; finally a black-cloaked shape was clinging to the sill.

A squdgy sound occurred as suction cups pressed against the brick wall of the deep courtyard. Hanging like a mammoth bat, The Shadow poised himself above the paving that shone white nearly a dozen stories below.

With regular motion, the strange figure moved along the wall until it reached a corner of the building. It turned, proceeded, and stopped close beside a window where light showed through a drawn shade. This window indicated the inner room of the suite occupied by Victor Venturi, who had registered as a resident of Naples, Italy.

A blackened hand appeared at the window. The sash moved softly upward. The hand dropped; the figure crouched and became invisible against the darkness of the wall. But through the tiny crevice at the bottom of the shade, two sparkling eyes peered into Venturi's room.

Two men were in view. It was easy to tell which was Victor Venturi. A short man of light build, with a hollow, sallow-skinned face, Venturi's dress alone denoted him as a man of culture. He was seated in a chair, nervously smoking a cigarette, and his quick, dark eyes were scanning his companion, another Italian of heavier build, but less intelligent physiognomy.

"Angelo," declared Venturi, speaking in Italian, "I am nervous to-night."

"You are always nervous, signor," responded the other man, in a matter-of-fact tone.

Venturi laughed glumly.

"You are an excellent attendant, Angelo," he remarked, "but at times you are too frank. However, you are correct. I am always nervous, and I shall be until these affairs are finished."

All this conversation was in Italian. It was evidently understood by the figure listening outside the window. For The Shadow still clung, invisible, to the brick wall.

"Why should you be nervous, signor?" questioned Angelo, in a soothing tone. "To worry is to be foolish."

"Right again, Angelo," responded Venturi. "Yet I cannot help but worry. Angelo, I have trusted you. You know my purpose here in America. You know that we may encounter danger. You can understand the suspense that grips me."

Angelo nodded.

"When I came here," continued Venturi, "I expected to receive orders that would enable me to visit certain persons on special business. Since my arrival, I have received new word from Monsieur Ponjeau. He has appointed an unknown agent in my place.

"Only one man, Angelo, should have the list of persons who must be visited. Those persons do not know each other. The one man has been appointed. He is visiting the persons now. I am the second fiddle."

"You have a duty, signor."

"Yes. I am to be given the names of those persons, one by one—after the time scheduled for the particular visit. One man has been seen. The work is accomplished. I await word that will tell me who he is. Then I shall visit him to make sure that all went well. Paugh, Angelo! That is no great duty!

"And while I wait, I must show caution. If there is danger, people will be watching me. Again, I am playing the second fiddle. Suppose there are enemies at work. What do they do? They watch Victor Venturi. They find out nothing. Even if they capture me, it means nothing. I am visiting stables from which the horses have been taken."

"You have visited none as yet, signor."

Venturi thumped his hand upon a huge stack of newspapers that lay on the table. His dark eyes flashed angrily.

"That is true, Angelo," he declared. "That is very true. It is why I worry. I await news from abroad. While I wait, I sit here and read newspapers that are printed in English. Paugh! But it is for a good cause, Angelo."

There was a knocking at the outside door. Venturi looked nervously at his servant; then made a gesture with his hand. Angelo left the room; then returned, carrying an envelope.

"A cablegram, signor," said the servant.

Victor Venturi seized the envelope and opened it. A coded cablegram came into his hands. He read the words eagerly.

"Here it is, Angelo!" he exclaimed. "The first man whom I am to see—to make sure that all was well when the secret envoy called. He does not live in New York, this man. He lives in the city of Hartford, Angelo—yes, he lives in Hartford. His name is Winston Collister—Winston Collister."

The cablegram fluttered from Venturi's hands. With a wild cry of alarm, the Italian seized the stack of newspapers upon the table, and began to run through them while Angelo looked on in astonishment. A minute later, Venturi was waving a journal before the eyes of his servant.

"Look, Angelo! Look! There is his picture—this man Winston Collister. A man who had millions of dollars. Slain in his home, only two nights ago!"

Throwing the paper aside, Victor Venturi paced up and down the room, sweeping his hands and tugging at his long hair with savage gesticulations. Angelo watched him with a perturbed expression and listened to his master's mutterings.

"Terrible! Terrible!" were Venturi's words. "This man is dead! The secret agent has failed, Angelo! Some rogue has gained what belonged to Monsieur Ponjeau! Terrible! I cannot go to Hartford now!"

Swinging, Venturi became suddenly stern. His troubled look turned to one of grim determination.

"That one is lost," he said solemnly. "Some terrible error has been made. But there are others besides that one. My duty now is to save our cause. Some evil man is at work. He will call upon the second of our friends as he called upon the first."

Venturi counted the fingers on his left hand and nodded thoughtfully.

"It may be to-morrow night," he asserted. "The evil man will be there. He will try to steal again—perhaps to kill. Monsieur Ponjeau must know. I must inform him. Let us hope that he can send me word in time, so that I may find the next man on the list before it is too late!"

Seizing a sheet of paper, Victor Venturi wrote a

coded cablegram. He folded the paper and gave it to Angelo.

"Send it right away," he ordered. "Be prompt, Angelo. To Monsieur Ponjeau—Aristide Ponjeau—Lausanne. It may enable him to inform me in time."

Victor Venturi continued to pace after Angelo had gone. The Italian emissary did not sense for an instant that eyes were watching him from the window. He was still walking back and forth when the servant returned.

"The cablegram is sent, signor," informed Angelo.

Venturi nodded. He slumped into a chair, and sat staring helplessly at the wall. Angelo, taciturn and motionless, stood at the side of the room.

There was a motion outside the window. The figure of The Shadow thrust a hand upward, and softly lowered the sash. The black shape moved back along the wall and stopped outside the window of Room 1108. After a brief interval of waiting, a hand came over the sill, and a figure slipped within the room.

A few minutes later, the cloak and other articles were back in the suitcase. A light glimmered by the writing desk. Henry Arnaud sat there, calm and unperturbed. Outside the room were whisperings in the hall. Henry Arnaud smiled.

As Henry Arnaud, he had come to the Dexter Hotel. He had deliberately incurred the suspicion of Bumps Jaffrey's men, so that he could have them under surveillance when he required. They would think of him as Henry Arnaud.

But, as The Shadow, he had done other work. He had visited Victor Venturi's room. He had learned the Italian's secret. He had connected Venturi with the murder at Hartford. He had linked the name of Crix, the supercrook, with the killing of Winston Collister.

Venturi now knew that crime was under way. The Italian would try to thwart the scheme of the man called Crix. To-morrow night, perhaps. All depended upon the arrival of a reply to Venturi's cablegram; and the Italian expected it surely.

The Shadow was ready to play a waiting game. As Henry Arnaud, guest of the Dexter Hotel, he could watch Venturi's room; and as The Shadow, he could visit that place when the time came. The conflict with Crix was now impending. Venturi would be the lead to the desired struggle.

Henry Arnaud went softly to the door of his room and silently closed the transom. Back to the desk, Arnaud lifted the receiver of the telephone and quietly called a number. A voice responded:

"Burbank speaking."

A whispered voice came from Henry Arnaud's lips. The Shadow was issuing instructions for the campaign that was due to come—a campaign which would have its inception in gangland's underworld.

CHAPTER XI

GANGSTERS START

Early the next evening, Cliff Marsland entered the Palace Havana and encountered Skeeter Wolfe. The cunning-faced gunman waved a greeting. Cliff took a chair beside him.

"Howdy, Cliff," said Skeeter. "Still stickin' around, eh?"

Cliff nodded.

"I saw Bumps Jaffrey last night," he remarked.

"You did?" questioned Skeeter eagerly.

"Yes," responded Cliff. "It guess he'll remember me when he needs me."

Skeeter smiled, and Cliff noted the expression. He could easily divine what was in Skeeter's mind. The gangster was going on a job with Bumps Jaffrey to-night. Skeeter's next action indicated that Cliff was correct.

"Gotta mosey along, Cliff," he said. "See you later."

When Skeeter had left, Cliff Marsland followed. Trailing Skeeter was not difficult. The man shambled to an "L" station, and Cliff followed him up the steps.

Watching from another car, Cliff saw the station where Skeeter stepped off, and did likewise. The gang-ster's shuffling steps led Cliff to a place that he knew well—the Hotel Spartan, on the Lower East Side.

It was here, singularly enough, that Cliff had first met The Shadow. Caught in a tight spot, Cliff had been pulled from trouble by the mysterious being of the night. After that, he had aided The Shadow in the war that had eliminated New York's most notorious racketeers.

Surrounded by dilapidated buildings, and located beside the roaring elevated, the Hotel Spartan now served as a meeting place for mobsmen. Here, Cliff knew, Bumps Jaffrey must be assembling his evil crew for a death-dealing thrust against an unsuspecting victim.

Cliff doubled back to the elevated station, paid a fare, and entered a secluded telephone booth. He called Burbank, and reported what he had learned. He received the instructions that he had expected; to stay on the ground and learn where Bumps and his men were going.

Returning to the vicinity of the hotel, Cliff peered into the lobby, where Skeeter Wolfe had gone. He did not see the shrewd-faced gangster; in fact, the lobby was almost deserted. There was a door at the rear, and Cliff, not wishing to be seen, circled to the back of the hotel to study the darkness of the narrow street. There, he made a discovery.

Three automobiles were drawn up against the curb, and a group of men were preparing to enter them. Boldly, Cliff sidled through the darkness, hoping that he could learn what might be going on. He was sure that this was Bumps Jaffrey's party; therefore, recognition was something that he desired to avoid.

Sneaking up behind the rear car, Cliff could hear the sound of Bumps Jaffrey's voice. All but two had entered the cars. Evidently, these were reserves who were to remain.

"Won't need you to-night, boys"—Jaffrey's voice was explaining what Cliff expected—"so you can scram. We're not coming back here. You know where to get hold of me."

Motors were purring up ahead. The sound of Jaffrey's voice was drowned. Suddenly, the gang leader's car pulled away, leaving Cliff Marsland in the open.

Quickly, Cliff ducked for the cover of the nearest wall. The two mobsters spotted him.

"Hey, you! What're you doin' here?"

Cliff's hand went to his pocket. His reply was to draw his automatic. He could not see the faces of the other men, nor could they see his; but the action of his arm was apparent. The gangsters reached for their own weapons.

Bumps Jaffrey's car was gone—and Skeeter, too, had departed. They, most of all, were the ones from whom Cliff feared recognition; but he did not want these others to remember him. Quick shots and a get-away—that was the only formula.

Cliff's gun spoke as revolver flashes came from the gangsters' hands. A bullet whizzed past Cliff's ear and plastered itself against the wall. One of the mobsmen dropped; the other dived behind a huge ashcan near the curb. Cliff's next shot resounded against the metal container.

The odds were even now; but only for a moment. A cry came from the gangster who had dived for safety. Glancing to the side, Cliff saw two men entering the street from the corner of the hotel.

Quick thought came to Cliff's aid. Springing across the street, he dived for the rear door of the hotel. Revolver shots followed him; but the bullet went wide. Plunging onward, Cliff reached the lobby. There, he stopped short.

A few minutes before, the place had seemed deserted; but the sounds of gun play had brought a quick change. There were half a dozen ruffians there now, and they blocked the path to safety. Revolvers flashed, and Cliff dropped back behind the door just in time to avoid the shots of the mobsters.

Cliff Marsland was in a veritable hornet's nest. He was between two forces of death; he instinctively chose the lesser. Three men were coming from the rear street—Cliff must fight his way through them.

Revolver shots at the Hotel Spartan meant gang war; and when one man was the sole objective, his chances were very small. As Cliff reached the back door, he saw a figure skulking across the street. A quick shot from the gun. A cry—then a groan as the man went down.

That shot brought replies—revolver flashes from two other places. A bullet skimmed Cliff Marsland's shoulder. With quick, prompt aim, Cliff delivered return shots with a vengeance. His markmanship was rewarded. His bullets reached the living targets. Cliff leaped into the street.

A shot came from the sidewalk. One of the wounded men had fired. Cliff felt a stinging sensation in his leg. A flesh wound, but it dropped him to the ground.

Leaning on an elbow, he fired quick shots at the spot where he knew the crippled gangster must be. There was no response. Cliff's bullets had gained their objective. The crippled gangster had met the fate he deserved.

As Cliff Marsland rose, he sensed that his momentary safety would gain him naught. He could barely stand, and he heard the shouts of gangsters who were coming from the passage at the rear of the hotel. Backing along the street, away from the corner, Cliff tried to take the long road to safety. His progress was slow and lame. He could feel the warm blood trickling down his ankle.

A crowd of vengeful mobsters burst from the door. The brilliant rays of a powerful flashlight revealed Cliff Marsland. In desperation, Cliff fired into the crowd. His gun spoke once: then clicked. The last cartridge had been used.

It was death now, Cliff thought, as he sank upon the curb, his wounded leg weakening beneath him. Within a second, a roar of murderous shots would end him. He could not even go down fighting.

The final roar of shots came—but Cliff, staring in amazement, saw that the flash came from the entrance of the alley. And it was directed at the flashlight, which was shattered to bits.

Some new arrival had opened fire upon the mob! Cliff, prepared for his finish, saw new hope in this rescue, for now he saw more than the blinding flash of gun fire. He saw the outline of a man in black, pumping the contents of two automatics into the astonished gangsters.

The Shadow!

He had come here in response to Cliff Marsland's report; in time to save his agent. Alone, he faced the mobsmen.

No one man could have withstood the fire of these angered scavengers. Cliff's hardy work had been useless against them before. Now the gangsters, in their turn, found their efforts useless against the superiority of The Shadow. Cries resounded, and staggering gangsters plunged back into the Hotel Spartan to save their hides.

The Shadow was moving forward now. Up to the door he came, and his automatics roared through the passage that led to the lobby. His leaden hail was driving the foiled gangsters into precipitous flight. The echoing shots died. Through the silence of the street came a long, mocking burst of laughter.

An arm gripped Cliff Marsland's shoulder. Cliff was drawn to his feet. Aided by The Shadow, he reached the end of the street, and felt himself pushed into the seat of a coupe. Then The Shadow was at the wheel. The car was rolling from the neighborhood of the Hotel Spartan.

Police whistles and sirens did not perturb The Shadow. The invisible being at the wheel of the coupe seemed to avoid the police who were coming to the scene of the fray. Cliff sensed the quiet whisper of the personage beside him:

"Report."

In response to that single word, Cliff quickly told what had occurred. Bumps Jaffrey and his mob were off on a job. That was all Cliff knew. The car drew up beside the curb.

Cliff Marsland rubbed his forehead and felt his wounded leg. He waited for The Shadow to speak again. No word came. Cliff stared suddenly at the seat where the driver sat. There was no one there!

The Shadow had gone, leaving Cliff in possession of the car. Cliff knew the answer. He was to use the car himsclf. Looking about to locate the vicinity where they had stopped, Cliff saw a sign in front of a nearby building, which read:

DEXTER HOTEL

Had The Shadow gone there? Perhaps. Wherever The Shadow had gone, it was not Cliff Marsland's duty to follow. The Shadow had his own missions. Cliff had done his best tonight. His work was ended.

In the driver's seat, Cliff found that he could run the car without great difficulty. The hotel where he was stopping was about thirty blocks away; it was a quiet place where he could enter without his limp being too conspicuous. He could order the car taken to the garage.

But as Cliff rode along, he could not help wondering, in spite of himself, whether or not The Shadow had gone to the Dexter Hotel.

Were new adventures brewing there; adventures which The Shadow would meet alone?

Only The Shadow knew!

CHAPTER XII

ON THE WALL

Henry Arnaud was back in his room at the Dexter Hotel. Seated calmly at his writing desk, he seemed a placid, lethargic individual. No one would have supposed that this man had just returned from a quick expedition in which he had overpowered a gang of desperate mobsmen.

Not only had Henry Arnaud—otherwise The Shadow—accomplished that superhuman feat; he had also managed to leave the hotel and return without exciting the suspicion of the men whom Bumps Jaffrey had stationed to watch him.

The point of observation which interested Henry Arnaud was the room on the adjacent side of the court, where Victor Venturi resided. Slight murmurs could be heard from the hall outside of Arnaud's room; but they were not disturbing. His main problem was that of paying another visit to Venturi's room, and Arnaud had purposely delayed the action, awaiting the psychological moment.

The battle in which Cliff Marsland had been wounded was the indication that important events lay just ahead. There was no time to be lost. Bumps Jaffrey had started on the expedition with a picked crew of gangsters. Cliff Marsland had failed to learn the destination. Clews might be obtainable at the spot where Bumps had started; but the same destination could be learned more effectively if Victor Venturi received the message that he expected.

Henry Arnaud arose from the desk and extinguished the light. In the darkness beside the bed, he performed the transformation of the night before, garbing himself in the somber raiment of The Shadow. His silent, gliding form emerged through the window, and made its hazardous way along the wall. The danger of a twelve-story fall was no deterrent to this phantomlike creeper.

The window sash raised at Venturi's room. To-night, the shade was more closely drawn; but a black-gloved hand lifted it with consummate care until there was space for the peering eyes. The scene within showed Venturi seated in a chair beside the table, nervously drumming with his fist. Angelo, sober and impassive, was watching his master.

The Shadow had arrived too soon. The expected cablegram had not arrived. To Venturi, these dragging minutes were endless. To The Shadow, who knew that danger was already in the making, they must have been even more trying; yet the black-garbed watcher waited with the utmost patience.

Almost as though it had been a signal, a rap occurred at the outside door of Venturi's room. The Italian sprang to his feet; then sent Angelo in his place.

The servant returned with an envelope. Venturi's fingers faltered as they tore open the envelope. Out came the message and Venturi, in his excitement, read it aloud in a low, tense voice.

"Ah! The name!" Venturi read slowly and carefully. "Sturgis Bosworth—in Montclair, New Jersey. We must go there at once, Angelo! Ah! We are fortunate. Montclair is not far from New York. But time is short, Angelo. It is to-night—that meeting. Come! Summon a taxicab. We are leaving immediately."

The window sash descended. The Shadow was on his return journey.

There was method in the action. A new danger had arisen, and only by promptitude could The Shadow ward it off. When Victor Venturi and Angelo left their room in haste, they would be well covered by watching mobsters, unless—

There was one solution. Those same mobsmen were concerned with Henry Arnaud. They could not perform a double duty. If unexpected developments occurred in Arnaud's room before Venturi and Angelo departed, the Italians could go on their way unmolested!

The task that lay before The Shadow was a most critical one. By suddenly creating a disturbance, he could draw the mob in his direction and, by a swift escape, head for the destination in Montclair in time to reach there before Venturi and his servant!

The Shadow's hands were gripping the window ledge of Henry Arnaud's room. A minute more, and the excitement would begin. Suddenly, those hands became motionless. Something had happened to block The Shadow's plan. A man was standing beside the window, peering into the darkness of the court.

As The Shadow waited, the man spoke in a low, gruff whisper, addressing other persons in the room. His voice revealed that he was one of the ruffians whose purpose at the hotel was to keep tabs on Henry Arnaud as well as Victor Venturi.

"I can't see nothin' out here," the observer growled. "There's a light over in Venturi's room; but I can't figure where this guy Arnaud went——"

As he spoke, the man stared downward. The gangster's gaze encountered the only spots of light that lay below him—the burning eyes of The Shadow!

In the space of less than a second, the staring gangster recognized the form below. He knew that he was face to face with The Shadow, the archenemy of crime.

To the most daring minions of the underworld, the name of The Shadow meant reality. The sight of a figure suspended on a sheer wall told this mobsman that he had met the one menace dreaded by all gangdom.

Hosts of gangsters had quailed when faced by The Shadow. This mobster was different. Not only one of Bumps Jaffrey's toughest gorillas, he was shrewd and quick of wits. He realized that he had gained the greatest advantage that any one could possibly hold in a meeting with The Shadow. Backed by others, all was in his favor. With a cry of triumph, the mobster broke the news and acted as he raised the shout.

"The Shadow!"

The mobster was leaning forward as he spoke, and a heavy revolver gleamed in his hand. With a ferocious swing, he brought the weapon straight downward, aiming a vicious blow at the head below him.

He was striking for the eyes—striking with all the venom that lay in his evil heart. His swing was made with fell purpose. When it landed, The Shadow would lose his hold and plunge to death below!

But as the gangster's arm descended, the hand of The Shadow shot upward. While one fist clutched the ledge of the window, the other caught the gangster's wrist and diverted the powerful stroke.

Despite the fury of the gangster's swing, The Shadow's clutch did not fail. The gloved hand gripped the wrist in viselike fashion, and the gangster, half through the window, found his bulging eyes staring squarely into the blazing optics that lay beneath the black slouch hat.

The Shadow's wrist moved in a powerful twist. The gangster clutched the window ledge with his free hand; then, as his grasp failed, he uttered an agonized cry as he felt his body turning.

His right hand lost its strength. The revolver dropped from nerveless fingers. The weapon shot downward into the court; and a half second later, the mobsman, making a last vicious effort to grapple with The Shadow, toppled in the same direction.

An agonized shriek sounded just as the revolver clattered on the paving. The shriek died like the passing whistle of a locomotive as the mobster plunged head foremost into the depths. He had fought The Shadow from a place of safety; the tables had turned, and he was crashing to his doom!

Oaths came from the room. The other gangsters had heard the cry of recognition; they had seen the brief, dramatic struggle at the window; they knew that their crony had been conquered by a superman.

With one accord, they leaped forward with drawn weapons, hoping, by a rain of bullets, to accomplish the deed which their companion had failed to execute.

Before a single gangster could find a target at which to aim, the free hand of The Shadow moved beneath the folds of the shrouding cloak. It appeared upon the ledge, and simultaneously the black-hatted head came into view. The eyes of The Shadow, piercing the darkness of the room, seemed to focus themselves upon the approaching gangsters.

One gunman fired. His haste destroyed his aim. A second, less hurried, laid finger upon trigger. A cannon-like shot resounded at the window. The aiming gangster fell. The Shadow's sweeping hand turned to the man who had fired first.

The Shadow's head dropped as his hand was aiming. Two shots seemed to leap at each other, one from the gangster's revolver, the other from The Shadow's automatic. The revolver bullet whistled through the top of the black slouch hat. The automatic's missile found its destination in the mobsman's evil heart.

"The Shadow!"

The cry was uttered at the door of the room. It was another shout of recognition from a gangster, and the answer to it left no doubt regarding the identity of the powerful adversary. That reply was a peal of mocking laughter; the sinister laugh of The Shadow. A strident, gibing burst of merriment, the pealing tones reechoed through the courtyard, a paean of victory that brought awe to those who heard it.

The conquering cry quelled the men at the door. The Shadow's laugh was as effective as a revolver shot. Hardened mobsmen who had invaded Henry Arnaud's room now scattered to the safety of the hall. There, in the outer light, they rallied as other men came running to their aid.

"The Shadow!"

With confidence in numbers, the gangsters burst into the room. Revolvers flashed and shots reechoed as the first of the invaders fired toward the window. A gangster switched on the light by the door.

A peal of laughter seemed to come from the wall itself. Standing midway in the room, his sinister form towering like the embodiment of doom, The Shadow was in the midst of his enemies!

The black-gloved hands were speedy and systematic. Their fingers pressed the triggers of the death-dealing weapons. The powerful .45s moved in a sweeping course, and before their wrath the mobsmen crumpled.

Only those who dived for safety, not daring to fire in return, managed to escape the leaden hail. Those of the dozen-odd mobsmen who tried to shoot The Shadow were balked by stern disaster.

Gun arms fell. Writhing bodies toppled to the floor. Answering shots were futile. One gunman, falling, pressed the trigger of his revolver before it slipped from his grasp. The bullet shattered a picture two feet from The Shadow's head.

Others met with the same barren result. Timing his shots split seconds ahead of his opponents, The Shadow rendered them helpless before they could do him harm.

The brief battle left half of the mob within the room. The others had dashed to the hall. There, they were fortifying themselves in doorways, still bold enough to remain, too frightened to attack. The last of the waiting mob had come to this spot. The six who remained were determined that The Shadow should not leave this room alive.

A low laugh came from the beleaguered room as the light went out. The Shadow had pressed the switch. His tall form was beside the window. Across the courtyard he could see that Venturi's room was dark. The two Italians had left just as the fight was beginning. The shots had drawn the entire mob in this direction, as The Shadow had intended.

Yet The Shadow's laugh was grim. Although his might had prevailed over that of the attacking mobsmen, the disadvantage at the beginning had rendered his original plan impossible. He had intended to carry the fight to the gangsters, not to await their attack. He had fought from the defensive. To step into that hallway would mean uncertainty. The Shadow must risk it; but he had met with serious delay.

Like a creature of invisibility, The Shadow moved across the room with feline stealth. His tall form stood beside the door. Out there, six gunmen were ready. Only a clever ruse could best them. The Shadow had faced situations like this before; but invariably, he tricked his adversaries by making them bide their time. To-night, time was short.

The eyes of The Shadow looked upward. They gleamed as they spied the transom above the door. Another second; the tall form was perched atop the head of the bed. The transom, guided by a cautious hand, was slowly opening.

An eye peered through the crevice. The muzzle of an automatic appeared beneath it. The waiting mobsters had not noticed this occurrence. The Shadow spied one gangster edged behind a corner of the hall.

The automatic roared. A cry came from the gangster's lips. The Shadow had clipped him. Again, the automatic blazed, and its reports brought hands into view.

The mobsters had seen the source of the shot. With

one accord, they flourished their revolvers in reply. All had the same objective—the transom. As the revolvers barked, shattering bullets smashed the barrier above the door.

These were killing bullets, had they reached their mark. But again, The Shadow was working on split-second schedule. With his first shots delivered, he had dropped to the floor before the rain of lead commenced.

An instant later, his eye and hand appeared at the door, through a narrow crack. Low, almost to the floor. The Shadow opened fire. Gunmen had come into view. With wild eyes upward, they were still hurling their barrage at the transom. The new shots, delivered from a spot six feet beneath, caught them totally unaware.

Cursing mobsmen fell before they could change their aim. Of the six, only two managed to elude The Shadow's wrath. They saw their comrades fall before they knew where the shots were coming from; instead of firing, they headed for a convenient stairway, just before The Shadow turned his gun in their direction.

The way was clear for the black-clad avenger. The Shadow stepped into the hallway. Shouts stopped him from further progress. A fusillade of shots came from the stairway. The fleeing mobsters had been met by new invaders. A second later, uniformed policemen entered the hallway from the stairs.

Here was a new and unexpected barrier to The Shadow. The delay had turned against him with a vengeance. The Shadow, avenger of crime, had no quarrel with the law. His purpose was to frustrate men of evil. Still, time was precious. He must gain his way unmolested.

Only one course offered. Back into the room. The door of 1108 slammed shut, and elated cries of the police bore witness to the fact that they had seen the action. The officers believed that they had encountered the ending of a fight between two mobs. They were determined to capture all the participants.

The key turned in the lock. The police stormed the door. The Shadow swiftly crossed the room and gained the window. Over the ledge went the black-clad shape. Again, the rubber cups squdged against the brick wall that surrounded the court.

Above the spot where one mobsman had fallen to his doom; back over the course which he had so hazardously traced before, The Shadow made his even way toward Victor Venturi's room.

The situation was serious now. Police were crashing at the door of 1108. The sound of the yielding barrier was plain. The door had broken with a splintering crescendo.

The police were within the captured room. Amid the shambles of dead and wounded mobsmen, they were searching for a living man. They found none.

The light was glowing in 1108. The head of an officer appeared at the window. The policeman's eyes scanned the walls of the court. They did not see the clinging form that had reached Venturi's window. Motion, then, would have meant betrayal. The Shadow rested, waiting through long, tense moments. At last came the cry that he had expected.

The policeman, glancing downward, had distinguished the body of the mobster who had plunged to destruction. He called out his discovery. Other heads appeared at the window.

"There he is!" was the shout. "Tried to get somewhere along the wall. Dropped to the bottom of the court——"

All eyes were in the one direction. The Shadow, beside Venturi's window, raised the sash. The shade wavered as the black-garbed phantom entered the room. A few moments later, The Shadow stood safely in the darkness.

The path was open now. From Venturi's room, around the corner from 1108, The Shadow could make a getaway. A stairway on the other side of the hotel—

a powerful car in a garage near by—a swift drive into New Jersey——

These were the steps that lay ahead. Yet, with all the speed that he might command, The Shadow faced an arduous task. Bumps Jaffrey and his men had started long ago. Victor Venturi had followed considerably later. The Shadow would be the last to make the trip. The delay had consumed the most precious minutes at his disposal.

These factors were the disappointments in the triumph of The Shadow. To him they meant more than the glory of victory over fiends. But in actuality, The Shadow had accomplished unbelievable feats since his return to the Dexter Hotel.

On the wall he had learned Victor Venturi's destination—the home of Sturgis Bosworth. On the wall, he had encountered and defeated the man who had tried to slay him. On the wall, he had opened the terrific attack that had downed an entire mob of hardened fighters.

On the wall, again, The Shadow had made his escape. The police back in the other room believed that they had accounted for all contenders in the gang war. They had not accounted for The Shadow.

A phantom of mystery, The Shadow had vanished from their very midst. Now, unscathed after two quick battles with men of the underworld, he was on his way to a new adventure!

CHAPTER XIII

CRIX CALLS

"A gentleman to see you, Mr. Bosworth."

Sturgis Bosworth looked up from his desk. He was seated in a private office that he had in his home at Montclair. He looked questioningly at the servant who had made the announcement.

"Who is it, Caleb?" he asked.

The servant handed Bosworth a card. It bore the name of Hugo von Tollsburg.

"Show him in," ordered Bosworth.

A few minutes later, the visitor entered the office. Sturgis Bosworth, like Winston Collister, found himself facing a man who had a foreign air, but who did not appear to be a German.

"I am Baron von Tollsburg," the visitor announced.

"Pleased to meet you, baron," responded Bosworth. "Sit down and have a smoke. Cigar or cigarettes?"

"A cigarette," said the visitor suavely, "but I prefer my own brand, thank you."

He lighted a cigarette, and the odor of Egyptian tobacco became noticeable in the room.

Sturgis Bosworth was a man past middle age, bald-headed, and serious in demeanor. He, like his guest, had lighted a cigarette, and as the smoke floated upward, Bosworth blew a puff and made a chance observation.

"It is an excellent evening," were his words.

"An evening which one might long expect," came the reply.

"With the world in turmoil——"

"—it is our duty to right it."

Sturgis Bosworth puffed again on his cigarette.

"I am glad that you have arrived, baron," he said. "I am ready to deliver the money to aid the cause of my friend Aristide Ponjeau. It has worried me a bit."

"You are providing a large sum," said the visitor, in a commending tone.

"It is not the money," returned Bosworth. "I have made millions through the manufacture of various types of machinery. I regard this contribution as an investment. The World Court of Industry will aid the international progress of big business. No, baron, I have merely been worried about the delivery of the funds."

"That worry is ended now."

Bosworth nodded in agreement.

"You have your credentials?" he questioned.

The man who called himself Baron von Tollsburg arose. He brought forth the same documents that he had shown to Winston Collister on the fateful night when he had slain the insurance magnate.

"These are satisfactory," announced Bosworth. "Your method is wise, baron—or should I say that Monsieur Ponjeau's method is wise? I—nor any of the other contributors—do not know the identity of those who are providing funds. We shall know later, however. It may prove surprising then."

Bosworth chuckled as he unlocked a desk drawer. He brought out an oblong box, and opened it to display a mass of bills of large denomination. He thrust a typewritten sheet across the desk to his visitor.

"Your signature, baron," he requested.

The visitor signed. He slipped his hand to his coat pocket as he saw Bosworth comparing the signed slip with the indelible signature upon the document. Sturgis Bosworth was not so close a scrutinizer as Winston Collister had been.

"This is quite satisfactory," said the manufacturer.

* * *

The false Von Tollsburg removed his hand from his coat pocket. He reached forward to take the box that contained the money.

At that moment, there was a knock at the door. The visitor looked up in momentary alarm. Sturgis Bosworth registered the same expression. With a lift of his hand, he went to the door.

"Who is it?" he questioned.

"Caleb, sir. A visitor. Quite important, sir. Here is his card."

Bosworth opened the door a trifle and received the card. His face paled momentarily, then regained its color. The millionaire laughed.

"It gave me a trifling shock," he said. "A visitor at this opportune moment. An old friend whom I have not seen for some time. He can wait."

"I shall be leaving immediately, Herr Bosworth."

"Of course. Of course"—Bosworth paused as he approached the desk—"but before you leave, baron, you must accept a special gift which I have provided for the emissary of Monsieur Aristide Ponjeau. Wait until you see it, baron. It will surprise you."

Bosworth reopened the desk drawer and fumbled as though looking for something that he had misplaced. Suddenly, his head popped up above the desk. His hand came with it, and an old-style revolver glimmered in the millionaire's fist.

"Put up your hands!" ordered Sturgis Bosworth, in a hoarse voice.

The visitor obeyed in feigned surprise.

"So! Bosworth's tone was indignant. "You have tried to trick me, eh? Well, it is fortunate that the next visitor arrived. Did you ever hear of Victor Venturi, Mr. Baron?"

The visitor registered blankness.

"He is a friend of Aristide Ponjeau," declared Bosworth. "He sent in this card that bears his name—marked 'From Aristide Ponjeau.' It also bears a written statement. 'Beware the impostor who is deceiving you.' What do you make of that, Mr. Baron?"

The visitor made no response. His hands still above his head, his eyes were gleaming in anger.

"You are an impostor," accused Bosworth. "Your face shows it. You have played into my hands. You have only one chance for safety. That is to play fair. Who are you?"

A slow smile showed on the accused man's face. He seemed to recognize the fact that he was trapped. Nevertheless, his tone was sarcastic as he replied to Sturgis Bosworth.

"I am not Baron von Tollsburg," he stated. "I may as well be frank with you before I face Victor Venturi. Von Tollsburg is dead. I killed him.

"My own identity? It might surprise you, Bosworth. I have more than one identity. You should therefore, be interested in the one that I have assumed for this particular work. I call myself Crix. Remember that name, Bosworth. Crix.

"An unusual name? Perhaps. Nevertheless, it is a good one. Shrewd crooks have obeyed Crix. He has always kept in the background. Smart men have known him only as Crix. I am Crix.

"Since you have learned my insidious identity, I may as well tell you more"—Crix, with a short pause, was rising as he spoke—"because it will mean much in your future life. Your future life, Bosworth, which will be very short.

"When Crix plots, Crix plots well. You may kill me if you wish, but the sound of your revolver shot will be your own death warrant. I have marked it as a signal for my men. They will leap to the aid of their master—to the aid of Crix. I am Crix, who killed Baron von Tollsburg, who killed Winston Collister. Crix, who will bring death to Sturgis Bosworth——"

The words broke off as Crix leaped across the table. He had caught Sturgis Bosworth at a moment when the man was tense because of the strange statements he had heard.

The millionaire pulled the trigger. The action was a moment late. Crix, in his swift leap, barely managed to strike Bosworth's arm aside. Coming over the table, the attacker grappled with the man who had tried to shoot him.

The struggle lasted only a few seconds. Crix, with a powerful blow, staggered Bosworth. The millionaire fell back, still clutching the gun, but before he could raise the weapon, Crix had drawn his own revolver. Firing point blank, he shot Sturgis Bosworth in the body. The millionaire sank without a groan.

Crix turned toward the door, a fiendish look upon his face. The door was opening, and the intruder saw Caleb, Bosworth's old servitor. The situation was identical with that which had occurred in Hartford. A servant coming to the rescue. Crix adopted the same alternative. With a fiendish smile, he pressed the trigger of his gun. Caleb dropped in his tracks.

Calmly, Crix pocketed his gun. He picked up the box and closed it. With absolute indifference, he stepped from the room and turned down a hallway that led to the side door of the house.

To-night, Crix had planned more carefully than before. He had spoken the truth to Sturgis Bosworth. The first shot was a signal. If it and the second had not been heard, the third had certainly carried to listening ears, for the door had been opened when Crix discharged it.

This getaway was easy. To-night the way to escape was guarded. Crix laughed fiendishly as he departed. Victor Venturi might be there; others might hear the shot within the house. They had been provided for. Turmoil was due to break within this home, and the strong hands of gangsters would be waging war for Crix!

Two million dollars was again the stake. Safely boxed, it was under the arm of the murderer, Crix!

Chapter XIV

THE SHADOW AIDES

Victor Venturi was pacing back and forth in the front reception room of Sturgis Bosworth's home. Nervous and perturbed, the sensitive Italian formed a marked contrast to his companion, Angelo, who was sitting silently in a high-backed chair.

The two had reached this residence after a swift ride in a taxicab. All the way to Montclair, Venturi had displayed his usual restlessness. He had prepared the card to be delivered to Sturgis Bosworth, and he was anxiously awaiting the outcome of the message.

Suddenly, Venturi ceased his pacing. He turned to his servant with a worried look in his eyes. The fact that Caleb, Bosworth's footman, had said that a visitor was with the millionaire, had caused Venturi to be unusually tense.

"What was that, Angelo?" quizzed the sallow Italian. "Did I hear a shot?"

Venturi's servant assumed a listening attitude.

"There it is again!" exclaimed Venturi.

A moment later, a loud report came to the ears of both men. The correctness of Venturi's claim was proven. A shot had undoubtedly been fired from the rear of the house.

"Come!" cried Venturi.

Followed by Angelo, the Italian emissary rushed in the direction from which the shot had come. He saw a hallway and an opened door beyond. Entering, Venturi stopped short as he saw two forms upon the floor.

Recognizing that the farther man must be Sturgis Bosworth, Venturi leaped forward and bent above the millionaire. He raised Bosworth's head, and saw the man's eyelids flicker. Dying lips moved.

"Crix"—Bosworth's voice choked—"his—name is—Crix—he robbed——"

The lips stilled. Sturgis Bosworth was dead. With an exclamation of wrath, Victor Venturi leaped to his feet and made toward the door.

"Our man has escaped, Angelo!" he cried. "Come. We must capture him!"

The Italian stopped short at the door. He was confronted by a hard-faced man who swung a menacing revolver. A motion of the weapon sent Venturi back into the room.

"So you're going after somebody?" came the question. "Take another guess, Venturi. You've got yourself to think about, right now."

Threatening faces appeared behind the man with the gun. Bumps Jaffrey was here with his gang. The leader of the hoodlums grinned as his mob advanced. Turning, Bumps spoke to Skeeter Wolfe.

"Take a look upstairs, Skeeter," he ordered. "If anybody makes a squawk, give them the works."

Skeeter left to follow instructions. Bumps, confident that there would be no interference, gloated over the helplessness of the victims who stood before him.

"Stand up against the wall," he commanded. "Move along—or you'll get some hot lead quicker than you expect it."

Venturi understood. Angelo, whose knowledge of English was limited, followed his master as Venturi backed slowly toward the wall. There was no mistaking Bumps Jaffrey's purpose. The gang leader intended to murder this pair in cold blood.

"So you were after somebody, eh?" questioned Bumps, with an evil leer. "You didn't know the guy was covered, eh? You wanted to get Crix, did you? Get Crix, eh? Well, you'll get the works instead!"

Bumps was threatening the victims with his revolver. Beside him were four gangsters. Another was standing watch at the door. Two murdered men were lying on the floor. Their dead bodies were the handiwork of Crix, the master crook.

Bumps Jaffrey laughed. Before he left, he, too, would have his toll of victims. The orders were to blot out Victor Venturi and whoever might be with him.

"It's curtains for you, Venturi," announced the gang leader coldly. "You pulled a swift one, to-night, getting away from my gorillas down at the Dexter Hotel. Maybe you were an ace there; but you're just a deuce spot here. Like some hot lead? All right. Try it!"

Up came the gang leader's revolver. Victor Venturi, despite the pallor of his face, stared into the muzzle of the gun. It was Angelo who quailed. The servant did not possess the fortitude of the master.

All eyes were upon the scene that foretold death. Only one man was keeping vigil—the mobster beside the door. He had seen death often. His duty was to watch. Nevertheless, he was lacking in his duty.

Occasionally, he glanced toward the room instead of looking along the hall outside. He admired the finesse of Bumps Jaffrey. That admiration was to provide his undoing.

There was a peculiar motion in the hall. A figure seemed to swirl from the darkness. It arose, a towering shape, beside the watching gangster. Turning to glance into the hall, the gunman stared into a pair of eyes that had materialized from nowhere.

Before a cry could escape the gangster's lips, a black arm struck downward. The barrel of an automatic crashed against the watcher's head. A gargling groan sounded in the man's throat as he crumpled to the floor.

Bumps Jaffrey heard that strange utterance. Instinctively, the gang leader swung toward the door. His henchmen followed his example.

Like the watcher, they saw the burning eyes. They recognized the form that had materialized in the doorway. The same cry came from five lips simultaneously.

"The Shadow!"

Bumps Jaffrey aimed his revolver toward the new menace. Two other mobsters flashed their guns. The pair closest to The Shadow made a leap toward the phantom shape in black. All these actions were futile.

A cannonade roared from The Shadow's .45s. Twice to-night, The Shadow had conquered hordes of gunmen. This was to be his third triumph.

The attackers who had sprung against them toppled. They had thrown themselves into the path of The Shadow's deadly automatics. Bumps Jaffrey stood helpless.

The gang leader's life had been saved only because his men had leaped upon The Shadow. They, instead of Bumps, had received the bullets from the automatics. With his other henchmen also attacking, Bumps dared not fire. He expected to see The Shadow fall. Nervously, he threw a cautious glance toward Victor Venturi and his servant, Angelo.

The roar of the automatics was repeated. Bumps saw his other men go down. Up came the muzzle of an automatic. The gang leader stared into the tube of death. Another second, Bumps would have fallen in his tracks. It was the unexpected arrival of Skeeter Wolfe that saved him.

Brought here by the sound of shots, Skeeter lunged from the hallway and threw himself upon The Shadow's shoulders. With one arm clutching at the black collar of The Shadow's cloak, Skeeter used his other to jab his revolver against The Shadow's back.

The gun barked, but it was discharged in vain. The Shadow, twisting away from the attack, fell from the point of Skeeter's gun.

At this juncture, Venturi made his first effort to save himself. He sprang forward toward Bumps Jaffrey. He grappled with the gang leader. In that action, he frustrated The Shadow's work.

The black-garbed fighter was upon the floor, where he had fallen with Skeeter Wolfe. His swift motion had sent Skeeter Wolfe sprawling; but The Shadow's automatic had not lost its aim. It was pointing up toward Bumps Jaffrey. Yet The Shadow did not fire, for Bumps had gained the protection of Venturi's body.

Skeeter Wolfe started to rise, clutching at his revolver, which was lying on the floor. With a sidewise motion of his arm, The Shadow delivered a stunning blow against the gangster's head. Skeeter flattened on the floor. The Shadow's automatic was swinging back toward Bumps Jaffrey.

Grappling with Venturi, Bumps had staggered toward the hinged windows. With a wild lunge, the gang leader leaped to safety. Head first, he crashed through the windows, which swung outward when he struck them. Amid the clatter of breaking glass, Bumps Jaffrey dived to the lawn outside.

The Shadow fired. For the first time to-night, his bullet was too late. Bumps Jaffrey had gained safety.

The gang leader was in desperate flight. Every one of his henchmen had fallen before The Shadow's might. Bumps, alone, had managed to escape—only through the fortune that had followed Venturi's thrust.

The Shadow had arrived in time to save Venturi. The Italian and his servant, Angelo, had been put on the spot. But for The Shadow's aid, they would have died. Bewildered, Venturi faced the strange personage who had rescued him.

"Come!"

The Shadow's word was a command. Beckoning to Angelo, Victor Venturi hurried toward the hall. Ahead, he saw the phantom form of The Shadow.

It was like a dream to Venturi, as he followed through the side door, where The Shadow led. A car was standing outside—a trim roadster, with softly purring motor. Venturi caught a glimpse of a beckoning arm in black. Without a moment's hesitation, he leaped to the wheel of the car, and drew Angelo in beside him.

Heading toward the street, Venturi drove down the driveway that led from Sturgis Bosworth's home. The Italian understood the situation now. Too late to save Bosworth's life; too late to confront the murderer; he, at least, had escaped, and could take for cover.

An envelope was tucked upon the steering wheel. At Venturi's low command, Angelo took it and opened it. The servant read the words of the note, holding the paper close to the dash light.

"It is written in Italian, signor!" exclaimed the servant. "It says to take this car to Markley's garage, on Fourteenth Street—to leave it there. It tells you to keep out of sight—otherwise there will be new danger. It says to warn the next man before the appointed night. You must learn his name from Monsieur Ponjeau. Ah! Here, signor, it names the place where you may be safe. Signor Folloni, Cafe Bella Napoli——"

Angelo paused to wave the paper excitedly. Aloud, he repeated the words that he had read while Victor Venturi nodded solemnly. Both Italians realized that this word was from the man who had rescued them; that he was a friend, who also desired to prevent crime, and to trap the enemy who had twice gained stolen millions.

Angelo's eyes went back to The Shadow's message. A strange ejaculation came from the Italian's lips. Staring, he saw the written lines disappearing word by word! As his eyes read through the message, each passage was wiped away as though by the action of an invisible hand.

Venturi, hearing the cry, dropped his gaze toward the

paper that Angelo held. In the light of the dashboard, he, too, viewed the unexplainable eradication.

If any doubt existed in either mind as to the amazing prowess of The Shadow, that doubt was now dispelled. The disappearing ink, in which the message had been penned, had been prepared according to The Shadow's secret formula. Its action, viewed by those who had never seen it, was uncanny. The paper in Angelo's hand was blank; but the message had left an indelible impression within the Italian's mind.

It was The Shadow's usual method of communication with his agents. Through it, and the simple code his agents knew, The Shadow's orders would be lost on others.

Later that night, two muffled strangers rang the doorbell of the Cafe Bella Napoli, an obscure Italian restaurant on an uptown street in Manhattan. They were received by Signor Folloni.

A squat, bearded Italian of middle age, Folloni bowed and conducted his visitors to rooms above the restaurant. In a low voice, he assured them that their identity would be concealed. A true son of Italy, Folloni was honored by the presence of so distinguished a guest as Victor Venturi.

The bearded Italian was taciturn. He did not state that he had been informed of the arrival of these guests through a mysterious phone call in which a weird, whispered voice had commanded him to perform this duty. Folloni had received a message from The Shadow. Its ominous tones and the mention of Victor Venturi had combined to bring from him a promise of strict obedience.

Later, the same night, Angelo returned to the Cafe Bella Napoli to report the execution of a secret mission. In the little room on the third floor, where Venturi awaited him, Angelo informed his master that he had sent a coded cablegram to Monsieur Ponjeau, reporting the new situation that had arisen.

Angelo's words were heard. Although a thick wall intervened between this room and the house beside it, all that was said was audible, thanks to an invisible wire that ran through the window and out along the wall. In the next house, a man was seated at a table, with ear phones pressed to his head, taking down phonetically each remark that was uttered.

Burbank, contact agent of The Shadow, had taken new headquarters. Although he could not speak Italian, Burbank was a marvel of efficiency. His phonetic notes would be repeated exactly as he heard them, when he contacted with The Shadow.

Another drama of crime was impending. Soon Crix would strike again. Victor Venturi would be sent to thwart him; once more the aid of The Shadow would be needed! Again, he would go back to the source!

CHAPTER XV

THE SHADOW HEARS

The little room above Duke's place was again occupied by two men who talked at the little table beside the wall. Bumps Jaffrey, gang leader, and Bart Shallock, confidence man, were in conference.

There had been no disturbance in connection with this meeting. Downstairs, Duke's speakeasy was quiet. No sweatered ganster had appeared upon the scene.

Nevertheless, The Shadow was again present. The location of this room was known to him. The windows opened at the inner corner of the alleyway; and there The Shadow had found an opportunity to arrive unseen and unheard.

A form of blackness, totally invisible as it moved slowly upward, The Shadow had reached the window immediately after Bumps Jaffrey had entered the speakeasy. The blackness in a corner of the room was the only token of his invisible presence. There, a thing of darkness, The Shadow listened as he had on that previous night.

The same subject held the attention of the speakers. The affairs of Crix, the supercrook, were of momentous consequence. Bart Shallock, suave and convincing, was buzzing words of confidence in Bumps Jaffrey's ear. The display of a stack of currency brought a pleased grin to the gang leader's face.

"Ten grand more," commented Bart Shallock. "There'll be plenty coming to you, Bumps."

"There ought to be," grunted the gang leader.

"Listen here, Bart. Another job like that last one is out. Get me? Out! I don't care what you offer me. I'm not taking chances with The Shadow."

"You're crazy, Bumps."

"Yeah? You're a great guy to talk. You weren't there. There's only one bird who could raise Cain the way that guy did. The Shadow—that's who it was."

Bumps nodded emphatically as he spoke. Bart Shallock shifted uneasily in his chair. The confidence man, despite his feigned disbelief, knew that Bumps Jaffrey was correct.

"Let me give you the lay, Bumps," offered Bart, resuming a smooth, purring tone. "Things went bad the other night—that's all. Now is no time to quit the game. I've heard from Crix again——"

"Yeah? Where is he?"

"I don't know. He talked over the telephone. But he told me more, and he wants you to stick. That's all. You've got to stick, Bumps. I'll tell you why.

"Crix is playing a smooth game. He had things fixed out there at Bosworth's. You and the mob were just waiting in case of a pinch."

"There was a pinch, all right," commented Bumps, in a sour tone.

"It was just a bad break," returned Bart Shallock. Venturi was the one that queered it. Somehow, he found out that Crix was in the game—that Crix was putting over a fast one. Venturi is a safety man; there's another guy supposed to be collecting dough. Crix is in on the ground floor.

"If your man had been on the job down at the Dexter Hotel, Venturi would never have got out to Bosworth's. But he got there—and he tried to queer the game for Crix. That left it up to you, Bumps. You had two things to do—help Crix make his get-away and hand the bump to Venturi."

"Well," growled Bumps, "Crix got away, didn't he?"

"Yes," responded Shallock, "but so did Venturi.

That's the tough part about it. There's no telling where he is. It's a sure bet that he will show up to spoil the next lay."

"I get you. More trouble for me, eh?"

"More work for you, Bumps. When I get the tip from Crix, you have the mob ready."

"The mob!" Bumps spoke in a disgruntled tone. "The mob's shot, Bart. Look at that mess down at the Dexter Hotel. I figure The Shadow must have been in that. Out at Bosworth's place—well, I was the only one that got away—no, Skeeter Wolfe managed to crawl out before the cops got there. Say, Bart—I can't dig up a bunch of gorillas to walk into The Shadow the way the others did——"

"Don't worry," said Bart Shallock suavely. "I don't know what Crix has in mind, but I do know he'll be ready for funny business this trip. Within a couple of days, he's going to show up on another job. When he gets there, he's liable to find Venturi. This will be your chance to get Venturi right.

"Use your head, Bumps. There'll be plenty of mazuma in it. We aren't taking chances, either. This time, Crix wants you and the mob to duck out of sight. Keep out of sight, until you get the word through me.

"Don't start from New York. Pick a hideout and keep the gang moving around from one place to another. You won't get the tip-off until you're needed. The Shadow—if he's mixing in it—won't be able to keep up with you."

Bumps Jaffrey nodded. This seemed like a good plan. The crinkling bills which the gang leader held were an incentive. Bumps could use more money.

"O. K., Bart," he said. "I'll have to move around now and begin to pick out some new gorillas."

"Get good ones."

"Leave that to me. I've got one bozo on tap who's a knock-out."

"Who is he?"

"Fellow named Cliff Marsland. Wants to work with me. I'd rather have him than half a dozen ordinary gorillas. He has brains."

"Are you sure you can get him?"

"Yeah. He drops in at Brindle's nearly every night. I'll see him there."

Bart Shallock smiled. He could see Bumps Jaffrey warming up. He knew that it was time to say no more. Rising, Bart clapped the gang leader on the back and walked from the little room. Several minutes later, Bumps Jaffrey followed.

There was a motion in the corner. The spectral figure of The Shadow emerged from darkness. The Shadow had heard. The Shadow knew. Crix, despite his narrow escape at Sturgis Bosworth's, was planning to go on with the game. This time, the supercrook would be more dangerous than ever.

Would the new adventure be similar to the last? Crix—Victor Venturi—Bumps Jaffrey—then The Shadow? Those four participants again would meet; but this time, circumstances would surely take a new turn.

A battle of wits as well as brawn was in the offing. Crix was preparing; so was The Shadow!

The tall form glided silently through the window. It disappeared into the darkness of the alley. Swallowed by the night, The Shadow had left to plan his campaign.

Less than an hour later, Cliff Marsland, strolling up Broadway, stopped to make a telephone call. He heard the voice of Burbank over the wire.

"Accept Jaffrey's terms," came Burbank's even order. "Forward all important information. Meet him at Brindle's to-night."

Continuing up Broadway, Cliff entered the cafe, wondering how The Shadow had learned that Bumps Jaffrey would be here with a proposition tonight. Cliff waited at a side table, and smiled to himself when he saw the gang leader enter and look about the restaurant. Bumps Jaffrey waved as he spied Cliff.

"Marsland," spoke Bumps, as he sat down at the table. "I've got a job for you. How about it? Want it?"

"Sure thing," responded Cliff.

The two men began a low discussion of terms. While they talked, Cliff still kept wondering how The Shadow knew. Where was The Shadow now? Cliff fancied that he might be near by, watching.

In this surmise, Cliff Marsland was, in a measure, correct. The Shadow was less than a dozen blocks away, moving silently through the darkness. But his objective was not Brindle's restaurant. The Shadow's destination was the darkened house that stood beside the building where the Cafe Bella Napoli was located.

The Shadow had listened in on Bart Shallock and Bumps Jaffrey. Now, he was to learn what Victor Venturi and Angelo were planning!

CHAPTER XVI

THE ANTIDOTE

A man was seated in a darkened room, a pair of ear phones close against his head. Burbank, quiet-voiced agent of The Shadow, was listening for words across the wire of a dictograph. The secret channel of communication with Victor Venturi's hideout was in operation.

Burbank did not detect the motion which occurred in the darkness behind him. His first knowledge that any one was in the room came when a smooth white hand pressed against his right wrist. Staring downward into the feeble glow that came from a switchboard light before him, Burbank caught the glimmer of a sparkling gem that seemed to flash shafts of fire.

The Shadow had arrived. Silently, Burbank arose from his chair and placed the ear phones on the table. He walked away and stood by the window, staring out into the darkness of a rear alley. There was a slight swish by the table as the cloaked form of The Shadow took the chair which Burbank had occupied.

Clicking sounds came through the ear phones. The Shadow was listening to words that came from the house next door. He could not see the faces of the men he heard; but he could understand their conversation. That, to this being of mystery, was sufficient.

In the low light of the room above the Cafe Bella Napoli, Victor Venturi was facing his placid-faced servant, Angelo. Despite his nervousness, Venturi was exhibiting a look of elation.

"Good news to-night, Angelo!" he exclaimed. "Wonderful news, which shall save our cause! Monsieur Ponjeau has taken sure action, and with my aid this evil enemy can succeed no longer.

"I trust you, Angelo, and I can explain what we shall do. I have been given the name of the next man of wealth who is to be visited. It is Roberts Faraday—his home is near a place called Southampton, on Long Island.

"There is a definite time, Angelo, when our agent is supposed to call upon Roberts Faraday. That time is Friday night, Angelo. That means that Friday night there will be trouble—I should say would be trouble, Angelo, but for Monsieur Ponjeau's plan.

"He has sent a special cablegram to Mr. Faraday, Angelo. It says that Faraday must expect a visitor on Thursday night—one day ahead of the time that was originally set. That visitor, Angelo, will be myself. I shall be there with my credentials, to give the warning.

"So when our enemy arrives, he will find an empty nest. You understand, Angelo? Some impostor is traveling about, purporting to be an emissary of Aristide Ponjeau. He was the one who was there before us, in that place called Montclair.

"We are safe, Angelo"—Venturi paused and laughed nervously—"we are safe, here at the Bella Napoli, with our new friend, Signor Folloni. Our enemy does not know where we are hiding. That is very good, Angelo, for this time we shall be ahead of him. We shall see Roberts Faraday first.

"But we must be clever, Angelo. On Thursday night, we must talk long and well with Mr. Faraday. We must discuss with him how we shall prepare to deal with our enemy when he comes—for he will be there for the money the night after us.

"He is strong, this enemy of ours, whoever he may be. He has assassins in his hire; he has slain two of our friends, and he has escaped with millions. He is poison, Angelo! Poison!" Venturi's face gleamed; then assumed a cunning look. "Poison! But we have found the antidote!"

Victor Venturi was silent. The Italian was thinking deeply. Angelo ventured a remark.

"The other night, signor"—the attendant's voice was solemn—"there was a man who helped us. I saw a man, signor—I mean that he was more than a man. He was a ghost, signor—a ghost in black."

Venturi nodded.

"His aim was timely, Angelo," he said.

"It was more than that, signor," added the servant. "It has been of use to us ever since. He wrote that strange message, signor—those words that went away before our eyes. It was through him, signor, that we came here to meet Folloni."

"Yes," responded Venturi, in a sober tone. "I know that, Angelo. It is our only danger."

"Our danger, signor?"

Angelo's question expressed immense surprise.

"Yes," repeated Venturi. "He was our friend that night, Angelo. But do we know that he will always be our friend? Perhaps he has a game of his own. There are millions at stake, Angelo.

"That strange man who rescued us was not an emissary of Monsieur Ponjeau. I, alone, should have the secret. Instead, I have discovered two who seem to know it.

"One—the man who murdered Sturgis Bosworth. Two—the person you have called the black ghost—who came to save us. Perhaps he is the enemy of the other. Because he saved us once does not mean that he will be our friend forever.

"We can trust no one, Angelo. No one but ourselves. That is why, on Thursday night, we shall be clever when we leave here. We will move so stealthily that no one—not even the black ghost—can discover where we have gone."

Angelo nodded with approval.

"You are right, signor," agreed the servant.

"We have the one man whom we know is an enemy," said Venturi, in conclusion. "He is the one who has been a murderer. It is you and I who must deal with him, Angelo, by warning Mr. Faraday. He is poison, Angelo, I am the antidote."

Victor Venturi repeated his simile with a firm conviction that impressed his faithful servant. The course by which the Italian emissary planned to deal with crime was plain and direct. Thursday night would bring the opportunity. Venturi would make use of it.

Confident, even though he did not trust the person whom he and Angelo had termed the black ghost, Venturi was sure that he would be capable of proper action. He was also positive that, although he and Angelo might be under occasional observation, no one could have heard this private conversation.

Venturi's beliefs were far from the truth. The emissary of Aristide Ponjeau did not realize the danger that confronted him. He did not know the power of the supercrook called Crix. It was fortunate, indeed, that The Shadow was a silent listener to this conversation.

Victor Venturi would work faithfully on the night of his meeting with Roberts Faraday, the third of the millionaires who had promised contributions to Aristide Ponjeau's gigantic plan for the stimulation of world industry. But between Venturi and Faraday lay the dangerous character called Crix—the man who had thrice committed murder before The Shadow could stop him—the man who even now had gained a place of safety which The Shadow had been unable to discover.

Crix was poison—in that statement, Victor Venturi had proclaimed an evident fact. But in terming himself and Angelo the antidote, Venturi had set forth a claim which the future was destined to disprove.

To so insidious a criminal as Crix, there could be but one antidote. Only the prowess of The Shadow could thwart the scheme of the fiendish supercrook who sought millions through cold and ruthless murder!

Crix and The Shadow. Their meeting was inevitable. When it came, one of the two would die! And it was coming soon!

CHAPTER XVII

MOBSMEN PREPARE

A group of men were seated in a basement room. Four were playing cards at a table. Six others, lounging about on benches by the wall, were growling among themselves as they expressed impatience at their enforced idleness.

One man, slouched in a corner, was dozing as though the tedium did not annoy him. Clad in baggy pants and heavy sweater, Cliff Marsland was playing his part as a member of Bumps Jaffrey's newly assembled mob.

Cliff held one leg outstretched upon a bench. This leg still bothered him a trifle from the wound that he had received several months ago, when The Shadow had rescued him at the Hotel Spartan. His limp, however, had not been noticeable enough to attract comment on the part of his gangster companions.

Some one thumped Cliff on the shoulder. Looking up, Cliff saw the grinning face of Skeeter Wolfe. With apparent indifference, Cliff closed his eyes and recommenced his doze.

"Gettin' on your nerves, Cliff?" questioned Skeeter. "Tired of waitin' around?"

"Not much," commented Cliff. "I don't mind loafing when I'm getting paid for it."

"You'll get paid for more than loafin', Cliff," said Skeeter, in a confidential tone. "Leastwise, you will if we run into anythin' like the last job. Some good boys took the bump that night, Cliff."

"How come?"

"You ask me? I'll give you the lowdown—an' you're the only guy I'd tell. The Shadow was there, Cliff. I tried to get him, but it didn't do no good."

"The Shadow? Humph!"

Cliff again closed his eyes. Skeeter stared with wide-open mouth. Finally, the gangster resumed his grin.

"Maybe you think The Shadow ain't much to worry about," said Skeeter. "All right, bozo. Have your think. I think different."

Cliff yawned and opened his eyes.

"What I want to know, Skeeter," he said, "is where we go from here. Bumps Jaffrey has been running us all over Long Island. Where are we heading? What's the lay?"

"That's Jaffrey's business," laughed Skeeter. "But you ain't the only one that's wonderin'. Listen to the rest of the mob. They're all askin' the same."

The buzz of conversation from the assembled mobsters proved the reliability of Skeeter's comment.

"Thursday night," declared Cliff. "Still on the move. I wouldn't mind meeting The Shadow and a dozen like him, Skeeter, if it would bring a little action."

"You'd get action aplenty," ridiculed Skeeter. "One guy like The Shadow is enough for me—an' a crowd beside. Pssst—here comes Bumps Jaffrey. Say—Cliff! That's Bart Shallock with him!"

Cliff Marsland looked up and saw the form of Bumps Jaffrey entering the room. Cliff studied the man who was with the gang leader. He noted the suave look on Bart Shallock's face. Cliff, despite his calm demeanor, felt a positive conviction that the time for action had arrived.

Since his introduction into Bumps Jaffrey's crew, Cliff had gained no inkling of the gang leader's purpose. The mob had moved from New York. Different spots on Long Island had been chosen as temporary quarters.

What was the game?

Cliff had tried to learn, without success. He had listened to the comments of the other gangsters. He had even conversed cautiously with Bumps Jaffrey whenever the chief gangster was present. To all appearances, no one—not even Bumps—knew what lay ahead.

Cliff had managed to communicate with Burbank on several occasions. Each time, he had given the location where the mob was staying. Instructions had always been the same—to preserve the utmost caution, and be ready for emergency. Cliff was positive that The Shadow knew the purpose for which Bumps Jaffrey's mob was being held in readiness. But, obviously, there were instructions coming from some one higher up.

Was that person Bart Shallock? So Cliff had supposed; but now, as he watched Bart and Bumps talking in a corner, Cliff had a sudden hunch that Shallock was no more than an intermediary between a hidden chief and the gang leader.

Had Cliff been able to overhear the conversation, he would have known the correctness of his supposition. But Cliff was too wary to approach. Hence he did not hear the words that passed.

"All set, Bumps," Shallock spoke.

"Crix is ready?" questioned the gang leader.

"Right," responded Bart. . . . "He's given me the lay. I'm going to place you and the mob."

"Where?"

"Southampton. Millionaire's house out there. All set for you and me to sneak in. We'll listen to what goes on—and the mob will be behind us."

"Who are we going to get?"

"Crix didn't say. We'll know, though. He's going to show up somehow, and we'll know when he gets there. It looks like we'll be after Venturi again, if I'm figuring right."

"Don't kid me, Bart. If Crix has given you the whole lay, spill it. I'll keep mum."

"I don't know a bit more," protested Shallock, in a

sincere tone. "There's going to be some sort of a meeting at a house near Southampton, and I've got the location of the spot. Crix has figured it so we can slide in. I've got the plan of the ground floor. We're to listen, and we'll get the lay."

"All right. Ready to go?"

Bart Shallock nodded as he heard Bumps Jaffrey's question. The gang leader turned and signaled to the gang. The mobsmen gathered around.

"We're going on to another joint," declared Bumps, in a noncommittal tone. "Stick together and keep quiet. We're going to slide into a place and lay low. That's all. And get this"—Bumps looked around with a challenging expression—"when I give the word to go, we go. Any rat that wants to squeak can try it. He'll only try it once. Remember, they call me Bumps! I'm just reminding you. Come on."

Cliff Marsland followed with the gang. They went out the rear door of the basement. This building was an old road house on Long Island, near the Sound. There was a telephone in the protected speakeasy upstairs, and Cliff desperately wanted to get to it.

But there was no turning now. He would have to wait for a later opportunity. Skeeter Wolfe was at Cliff's elbow. There was no chance to slip away.

Cars were waiting. Cliff clambered into an old sedan, with Skeeter still at his elbow. The cars started off. Cliff kept a close watch on the road. It was not long before he decided where they were bound for—Southampton, most likely, or beyond that.

How could he inform The Shadow? During the past few days there had been opportunities. Those had been times when there was no information to give. Now, when a report was vital, Cliff could not find the way.

He was still counting up his chances when the cars swerved from the highway, and formed a short procession as they turned into a narrow lane.

The machines drew up beside a high hedge. Bumps Jaffrey, a flashlight in his hand, was counting noses. He spotted Cliff and Skeeter, and ordered them to alight. Soon the entire mob was gathered beside the hedge.

"Easy now," ordered Bumps, in a gruff whisper. "Move along. Follow Bart Shallock here."

This was the first statement as to Bart's identity. With Skeeter nudging him, Cliff moved along among the first gangsters. Bart Shallock was using a small flashlight to indicate the way along a narrow path that broke an opening through the hedge.

A dimly lighted mansion stood in the midst of a rolling lawn. Bart's course was circuitous as he drew the gangsters toward a side wing, where a glow came from windows that were close to the ground. As they neared the house, Bart flicked his light in a warning to stop.

A flight of stone steps lay directly ahead. These led downward, into the lower portion of the house. Bart Shallock pointed to the steps, and spoke in a low tone to Bumps Jaffrey, who had just come up from the rear.

"Put some men in here," ordered Bart.

Bumps picked out two gangsters, and told them to keep guard on the steps. The men dropped out of sight into convenient spaces at each side. They were firmly entrenched, and Bumps gave a grunt of approval.

Cliff Marsland appreciated the effectiveness of the position. Any one approaching the side of the house could be immediately covered by these gangsters.

Bart Shallock descended the steps and tried the door. It opened at his touch. He clicked his flashlight, and moved it momentarily as a sign for the others to join him. Bumps urged the mobsmen down the steps.

Cliff, still near the head of the gang, found himself in a short corridor that led from the main portion of the house into the wing. There was a room directly across the hall, and another to the left. Both doors were closed; the room at the left was apparently the one which was lighted.

"Come on."

Bart was whispering. The mobsters crossed the hall, and Bart opened the opposite door to usher them into a dark room. When all were there, he closed the door behind him.

"Put two men at the door we just came through," he told Bumps.

The gang leader picked out two mobsters. Cliff hoped that he would be one of the chosen pair. He was disappointed. Bart walked over, and gave the men whispered instructions.

Taking temporary command, Bart Shallock then posted the remaining men about the center of the room; flickering his light, he showed a door at the rear.

"That leads to the back room," explained Shallock, in a voice just loud enough for all to hear. "There's going to be some people in there later to-night. Bumps and I will be watching. You men at the hall door be ready to cut off any guy that tries to get away. The rest of you be ready to bust into the back room when Bumps and I give the call."

As a last action, Bart Shallock went back into the hall, and opened the outer door. They could hear him speaking to the gangsters who were posted outside.

"Keep watch," were his orders. "Nobody gets in here, see? And when trouble cuts loose inside, nobody gets out. Understand?"

A gangster's growl came in the affirmative. Then came a cautious voice.

"There's a car comin' up through the driveway——"

"Sh-h!" Shallock's warning was a quick one. "Time to be ready."

The confidence man closed the outer door, and hurried across the hall. He closed the door of the room until just a tiny crack remained open, so that the waiting gangsters could peer through. He joined Bumps

Jaffrey at the door to the rear room. Here, also, Bart opened the door just a trifle.

This time, Cliff Marsland, slipping closer in the darkness, could hear what Bart Shallock said to the gang leader.

"We're all set, Bumps," was the confidence man's statement. "This is the way Crix told me to fix it. He knows what's coming off here to-night. He'll get in through the front—like he did out at Bosworth's, I guess. Anyhow, I'll know when he gives the tip-off. The guy that owns this place isn't home yet—maybe that's him coming in by car. Anyhow, we'll be set when we're needed."

"Even if we have to bump off The Shadow," said Bumps grimly.

"Don't worry about The Shadow," commented Shallock. "Leave it to Crix."

Crix!

The name flashed through Cliff Marsland's mind. He had been on the lookout for an underworld character with an unusual name; later, Burbank had instructed him to listen constantly for word of a man named Crix.

Crix!

The man must be a supercrook. The one whom The Shadow wished to thwart.

More than ever, Cliff Marsland wanted to make his report. It was too late now. He could not possibly get away from here.

Crix was behind this job to-night. Crix plotted crime and death. Crix had a mob of a dozen men in readiness.

Death!

It might threaten Cliff himself to-night. But whatever might come, The Shadow's agent was in readiness. He was sure that he could not count on The Shadow now. He had failed to relay news of this expedition to his mysterious chief.

But when the crisis came, Cliff would fight to the end. He would do his utmost to frustrate the evil work of Crix, even though he would have to turn his guns upon the dozen men who formed Bumps Jaffrey's gang.

To reveal himself as the enemy of this evil crew would surely be a fatal step; yet Cliff planned that very action, in the service of The Shadow!

CHAPTER XVIII

FARADAY'S VISITOR

Footsteps sounded along the hall that led by the door where a pair of watching mobsmen lay. A man in evening dress walked by, followed by two servants. He opened the door of the rear room, and entered the lighted chamber.

Roberts Faraday, the millionaire, had just returned from New York City. The uniformed men who accompanied him were his house man and his chauffeur. Seating himself at a huge desk in the middle of the lighted room, Roberts Faraday looked at his servants.

The millionaire was a man of about forty years. Firm-faced and businesslike in appearance, he showed power and dominance in every expression. His smooth-shaven countenance was marked by the sternness of his eyes. Roberts Faraday was unquestionably a man of forceful character.

"Crayle"—Faraday was addressing the butler—"I am expecting a visitor shortly. His name is Victor Venturi. When he arrives, show him in here. Then you can leave. Boggs"—Faraday was referring to the chauffeur—"will wait for you and drive you back to the city. I shall remain here to-night."

"Very good, sir," said the house man.

"You have been here all evening?" questioned Faraday sharply.

"Yes, sir," responded Crayle. "I—I was dozing, sir, up in the front hall. Waiting for you, sir——"

"That's enough. You may go. You too, Boggs."

Roberts Faraday arose after the two left. He strolled back and forth across the room. He did not chance to glance toward the door that led to the next room. Hence he did not see that it was ajar. Once, in his pacing, Faraday turned and looked toward the rear wall of the room. Set in that wall was the steel door of a large vault—the most formidable type of strongroom that modern ingenuity had yet devised.

There was something in Faraday's step that indicated repressed nervousness. The millionaire glanced at his watch, and noted that the hour was nearly midnight. He went back to his chair, extracted a cigarette from a case, and lighted it. Smoking seemed to ease his impatience.

When he had finished his cigarette, the millionaire opened a desk drawer and drew out a sheaf of documents. He went through them one by one. He gave particular notice to a cablegram that was on top of the pile. The name at the bottom of the message was that of Aristide Ponjeau.

Minutes ticked by. Faraday, smoking another cigarette, watched the clock while he waited. The hands reached twelve. The clock chimed the hour. Long, tense seconds passed; then, as if in answer to the millionaire's expectations, a distant ring came from another portion of the house. Someone had rung the front doorbell.

Time seemed long before the inevitable result occurred. Footsteps echoed from the hall. Crayle, the house man, appeared and advanced across the room. He stopped short, and made the announcement that Faraday awaited.

"Mr. Victor Venturi, sir."

"Show him in here, Crayle."

"He is not alone, sir."

"No? Who is with him?"

"His attendant, sir—an Italian gentleman. Mr. Venturi explained that he is always accompanied by his man."

"That will be all right, Crayle," said Faraday, in a thoughtful tone. "Bring them both here. I shall be waiting."

Crayle's footfallls echoed into the distance of the long hall. A few minutes later, mingled pacings could be heard. Victor Venturi, sallow and nervous-faced, entered, with Angelo at his heels. Crayle was behind the two. He stopped at the door.

"Ah! Mr. Faraday!" exclaimed Venturi.

Roberts Faraday had arisen. He extended the hand to the Italian; then looked questioningly toward Angelo.

"My attendant, Mr. Faraday," explained Venturi. "Angelo is always with me. It is quite all right for him to be here."

Venturi spoke in careful, musical English, choosing his words with much thought. Angelo stood by, offering no comment. It was obvious that the attendant knew very little of the language which his master was using.

"You may go, Crayle," said Faraday brusquely.

The house man bowed and went away. Faraday listened intently until he heard the footsteps reach the end of the hall. He continued to listen; at last the throb of a motor came from outside the house, barely audible to the millionaire's ears. Faraday motioned Venturi and Angelo to be seated. He took his own place behind the desk.

"You came here by taxicab?" questioned the millionaire.

"From the station, yes," responded Venturi.

"Good," commented Faraday. "We are entirely alone. My servants have gone for the night. I thought it best—in view of our private negotiations. I can summon a cab when you are ready to leave."

The millionaire reached into his pocket and produced his cigarette case. He held it open toward Venturi and Angelo; both shook their heads. Faraday withdrew a cigarette for himself, and lighted it. Then, calmly to Venturi:

"You have your credentials?"

The Italian bowed.

"I have," he said. "They are here, sir."

Venturi brought the papers from his pocket. Roberts Faraday examined them. Signed by Aristide Ponjeau, these documents were similar to the ones which Crix, as Baron von Tollsburg, had used to trick Winston Collister and Sturgis Bosworth into giving him their millions.

The second sheet, however, bore the signature of Victor Venturi, instead of Hugo von Tollsburg. Roberts Faraday did not have time to ask for a verification of the indelible signature. Victor Venturi produced a pen and sheet of paper. Leaning upon the desk, he wrote his name. Faraday compared it carefully with the signature on the document.

"You understand, of course," explained Venturi, "that my mission here is purely one of warning. It is not my province to make a request for money. We can discuss that matter afterward. It is because of unexpected occurrences that I have come to you——"

Roberts Faraday waved his hand in an impatient gesture. He was still comparing the signatures. His sharp eye did not let a single detail slip. Venturi stood silent until the inspection was completed. Quietly, Faraday gave the documents back to the Italian.

"The cablegram from Monsieur Ponjeau warned me," Faraday explained. "That was sufficient. It made me decide to use the utmost caution. I am an expert on signatures, Mr. Venturi. Yours has passed a most critical test.

"I am satisfied. You are an emissary from Aristide Ponjeau. Be seated, sir, be seated. I must hear your story. I realize that it is most important."

Victor Venturi resumed his chair. With back to the door the Italian faced the millionaire. The two men were intent; Angelo was watching them with all attention. Facts were to be revealed—and behind the partly opened door of the adjoining room keen enemies were listening.

Victor Venturi and Roberts Faraday were conferring within earshot of the evil men who served the arch-villain, Crix! Twelve armed men were waiting; and only one, Cliff Marsland, was there in The Shadow's service!

CHAPTER XIX

VENTURI EXPLAINS

"I shall start from the beginning, Mr. Faraday," declared Victor Venturi, in a methodical tone. "It is wise that I should do so. Matters have arisen that make clear understanding highly important. You—yes, you as well as I—are confronted by grave danger.

"This danger, Mr. Faraday, involves the future of Aristide Ponjeau's great dream—the World Court of Industry. Millions are at stake, my friend, and it is our duty to save them."

"I divined as much," interposed Faraday. "The cable from Ponjeau told me that danger lay ahead."

"One year ago," continued Venturi, "Monsieur Ponjeau, realizing that international cooperation would be necessary to world-wide prosperity, came to this country and visited ten men of great wealth. Each of those men promised to contribute two million dollars to the cause. The names of those men were not known to one another.

"The original intention of Monsieur Ponjeau was to visit the United States himself and obtain the money. He later decided to send me as his emissary. I came to New York. Here, I was to receive the list of millionaires; to visit each by appointment; to receive the funds from them.

"However, Monsieur Ponjeau again changed plans, almost at the last moment. He informed me that he had another emissary, a man in whom he had the utmost trust. He stated that this man was able to enter the

United States unseen; on that account, it would be preferable for him to make the collections. Monsieur Ponjeau feared that some enemies might have divined his plan.

"A new mission was intrusted to me. I was to visit these millionaires after the collecting emissary had called. I did not learn the names; I was to receive them one by one after each had been visited. The first name was sent to me. I was amazed when I learned it. Winston Collister. That man had been murdered in his home a few days before!

"I informed Monsieur Ponjeau that something must have gone wrong. He sent me the name of the next man on the list. Sturgis Bosworth. I hurried to the man's home. The fiend was there before me! Sturgis Bosworth was dead; I barely escaped with my life, for the fiend had placed assassins there to kill me!

"Since then, Mr. Faraday, I have been in hiding. I notified Monsieur Ponjeau. He sent me your name. He arranged an appointment before our enemy could reach you. This is Thursday; the fiend will not come here until to-morrow."

Roberts Faraday nodded thoughtfully.

"Yes," he said, "that is the time set for the appointment. I have been preparing for his visit. You are twenty-four hours ahead, Signor Venturi. But you come here merely to forestall—not to solve—the difficult riddle that confronts us."

"I have come to confer."

"Exactly. But how does that help us? Do you know the name of the criminal who has caused this trouble?"

Venturi shook his head.

"Then," declared Faraday, "four millions of dollars have already been lost beyond recovery."

"No!" exclaimed Venturi. "I cannot believe that those funds are irretrievable. If we can intercept our enemy to-morrow night—perhaps we can turn the tables upon him, Mr. Faraday!"

It was Faraday who now shook his head.

"From what you say, Signor Venturi," he remarked, "this enemy knows that you are upon his trail. You encountered him at Sturgis Bosworth's. You managed to escape his toils. He will be a thousand times more wary to-morrow night——"

"Yes," interrupted Venturi, "but you will not give him the millions. There must be no money here. We must lay a clever snare. You understand?"

"He will suspect a snare," stated Faraday. "How do you know, Signor Venturi, that he will come here at all? Perhaps he will eliminate me from the list——"

"Ah, no! He does not dare! He must keep each appointment; otherwise some waiting man might communicate with Monsieur Aristide Ponjeau. You see? I am trying to consider it from the enemy's view——"

"He may be satisfied with the four million that he has already taken."

"Let us hope so," stated Venturi quietly. "Then the sixteen million will still be ours. Ah, Mr. Faraday, I have thought long upon this. Our enemy cannot afford to miss a single link in the chain. To-morrow night will be the crisis. If our enemy fails to appear at this house, it will be a sign of his weakness—an admission of defeat. We can charge four millions as a loss, and I can arrange to collect the rest of the contributions.

"But if he does appear here"—Venturi's nervous face became tense and grim—"then it must be a battle to the death. Not only must we end the career of this fiend; we must also try to recover the funds that he has already stolen. Think of it! Monsieur Ponjeau's dream of international prosperity—about to become a reality—shattered by a murderer!"

Robert Faraday held up his hand in interruption.

"Signor Venturi," he declared, "we must not overlook any possibility. We are dealing with a shrewd schemer. You are right—we must prepare for him, to-morrow night. If he comes, it will mean a battle; but if he fails to come—what then? How will you proceed?"

"I shall notify Monsieur Ponjeau," stated Venturi. "Look, sir"—Venturi paused to draw a paper from his pocket—"this is the very cablegram that I shall send him. It says: 'The chain is broken. All is safe.' In return, I shall receive the names of the other men, one by one. I shall become the new emissary. With my credentials, I shall go the rounds, in place of the man who was slain."

"But if the enemy reappears?"

"I shall be prepared for him. Monsieur Ponjeau places full reliance in me; but he will take no chances. When he receives this message, he will dispatch secret agents to aid me. They will be on hand—watching—guarding—ready to frustrate all enemies. We did not need them when we thought that secrecy was in operation."

"I understand," said Faraday, with a nod. "You are alone at present; but you can obtain powerful aid. This cablegram covers matters if the crook does not appear. But suppose, Signor Venturi, that you and I are able, to-morrow night, to apprehend this man whom you term a fiend. Suppose that we should end his evil career?"

Victor Venturi's eyes were gleaming at the happy thought. From his pocket, he drew forth another paper and showed the message to the millionaire.

"This coded message," explained Venturi, "states that our enemy is dead. I hope to send it to Monsieur Ponjeau, to-morrow night. Should Monsieur Ponjeau receive this message, he will leave all to me. There will be no need for secret agents to protect me. I shall simply keep the regular appointments upon receiving the list from Monsieur Ponjeau.

"Upon receiving the list"—Venturi was repeating the words slowly—"unless I do not need the list. It would be my delight, Mr. Faraday, to take the credentials and the list from the fiend himself. He will have them with him if he comes here to collect your share to-morrow night."

"If he comes to-morrow night," said Faraday softly. "Do you think, Signor Venturi, that he might come *before* to-morrow night?"

Venturi's brow clouded. This suggestion was something that the Italian had not considered. Venturi shifted uneasily in his chair; despite his optimism, he was forced to consider the possibility that Faraday had offered.

"We are in danger," added the millionaire. "If the enemy has watched you closely, Signor Venturi, he may know that you are here at present. You have explained important facts to me, signor; I, in turn, shall explain some to you.

"I received a letter from Monsieur Ponjeau yesterday. He mentioned matters which I was instructed to tell to you. Acting upon his information, I was fortunate enough to gather additional data. I shall tell you, now, the exact dangers which we face."

From a desk drawer, Faraday withdrew several sheets of crinkling paper, in different sizes and colors. Referring to these documents, the millionaire began to speak in a calm, steady voice. Victor Venturi listened to the words in amazement.

Other men were listening also. Bart Shallock and Bumps Jaffrey were in readiness, beyond the door—waiting there, to serve the cause of Crix!

CHAPTER XX

ENTER CRIX

"My wealth," began Roberts Faraday, glancing steadily at Venturi, "has been gained through a knowledge of international affairs. It was because of my reputation for big business transactions with foreign countries that Monsieur Ponjeau came to me. He felt sure that I would be interested in the development of his World Court of Industry.

"I agreed to aid Monsieur Ponjeau. I also warned him. Well did I know that there were sharp men of crime who would be ready to prey upon his plan. In addition to my warning, I also made investigations for my own protection. I learned the identity of a super-crook whom we well might fear.

"You understand, signor, that I travel frequently abroad. In fact, I but recently returned from such a trip. Knowing my ability to detect the plans of schemers, Monsieur Ponjeau, in this letter"—Faraday was raising one sheet of paper—"told me the measures that he took to send a secret emissary to the United States. That information, signor, fits in with facts that I had gained regarding the cleverest of crooks. The man whom we must fear, signor, is one who calls himself Crix."

Venturi blinked as he heard the unusual name. It was evidently new to the Italian. The door across the room moved slightly. Venturi did not see it, for his back was turned. Roberts Faraday, on his part, was glancing at the papers which he held in his hand.

"Aristide Ponjeau," resumed Faraday, "had, as a

trusted aid, a German named Baron Hugo von Tollsburg. Months ago, Ponjeau planned to send Von Tollsburg to the United States to serve as his secret emissary. He had left the preparations to Von Tollsburg. The German, through his friend, Captain Heinrich von Werndorff, planned a secret trip aboard the dirigible *Munchen.*

"Baron von Tollsburg set out upon that voyage. He carried credentials, and the names of the men whom he was about to see. Smuggled safely into America, he would be able to act without molestation. But something has gone wrong. The crook who is making the collections has been doing so as Baron von Tollsburg.

"A traitor?" hissed Venturi.

"Von Tollsburg?" questioned Faraday. "No, signor, I believe that the German was honest. He would not have been forced to kill Winston Collister in making the first collection. There is only one solution. The true Von Tollsburg never reached America. His plans were discovered by none other than Crix.

"We can be sure that Crix was aboard that dirigible also. He slew Von Tollsburg. He took the baron's papers. He—Crix—visited Winston Collister, and later, Sturgis Bosworth. They were the first two upon Von Tollsburg's list. I, signor, am the third."

"And therefore Crix——"

"Crix is seeking millions."

"He may come here to-morrow night!"

"He will be here to-morrow night," responded Faraday, in a quiet tone. "A man of his ability—one whose identity is entirely unknown—will miss no opportunity. Crix has gathered four millions already; he will not balk at the chance to gain the wealth that still remains at large."

"Crix!" Venturi repeated the name. "Crix—you are sure that he is the man who has done these crimes?"

"I am positive of it," said Faraday, referring to the papers, and shifting them in the stack.

"Crix!" again repeated Venturi. "You are sure he is the enemy. But who can the other be—the one who aided me in my escape—the one who sent me to the Cafe Bella Napoli?"

Roberts Faraday looked up, a questioning gleam in his eyes. This was a matter that Victor Venturi had not mentioned before. The Italian saw Faraday's look, and hastened to explain.

"Evil men were about to slay me," said Venturi. "Then came the man in black—'a black ghost,' Angelo called him. He shot down those who threatened me. He sent Angelo and myself away in an automobile—to a hiding place above a restaurant—the Cafe Bella Napoli."

"Ah!" exclaimed Faraday. "You say that this occurred at Bosworth's home?"

"Yes."

"A man in black"—Faraday paused to consider—"who looked like a black ghost. A living ghost, you call him. There again, Signor Venturi, my knowledge of crime can offer an explanation. There is a man who fights crime—a strange personage of mystery—who calls himself The Shadow.

"He is the one who came to aid you. There is no doubt about it. The Shadow is opposed to Crix. Since The Shadow was at Bosworth's, The Shadow may be expected here—to-morrow."

"Then if Crix is here——" Venturi blurted the words.

"Crix will be here," responded Faraday, in a confident tone.

"Ah! You feel sure of it?" questioned Venturi. "Then, this time, Crix may meet The Shadow!"

"Yes," said Faraday, "and that is why we must be careful. Strange developments have caused two supermen of differing purposes to cross their paths. You, Signor Venturi, are but a plaything in this drama of crime and warfare. Millions are at stake, and it is beyond your power to preserve them.

"To-morrow night will be the crisis. I foresee a mighty struggle. It is not a question of your ability to frustrate the plans of Crix. The question is: can The Shadow do so?"

Victor Venturi sat like a man in a daze. These amazing revelations had come so suddenly and from so unexpected a source that the Italian could not understand. Crix—he had never heard the name before, yet he was convinced by Faraday's quiet tone that the man must be the murderer in back of all these crimes.

The Shadow—there was a fantastic thought—yet Venturi realized that such a personage was also existent. He and Angelo had seen The Shadow!

This interview with Roberts Faraday had proven bewildering. Nervously, Venturi surveyed the millionaire. Faraday was resting back in his chair, lighting another cork-tipped cigarette. The millionaire's confidence was nerve-racking to Venturi. With sudden excitement, the Italian raised his hands in gesticulation.

"You are sure," he questioned in an incredulous tone, "that all these facts are true? You have the proof of them?"

In reply, Roberts Faraday passed the sheaf of papers across the table. Venturi seized them eagerly.

The top sheet was blank. Venturi tossed it aside, and looked at the blue sheet to which Faraday had referred as Ponjeau's letter. That sheet was blank also!

"There is nothing here!" exclaimed Venturi. "What can this mean? You have been reading from nothing! You have told me of a man called Crix—Crix—who is Crix?"

The Italian stared toward the man behind the desk. Roberts Faraday had arisen. From a desk drawer he had drawn two revolvers. With one weapon in each hand, the millionaire was covering Venturi and Angelo.

A fiendish smile had come over Faraday's lips. The man's eyes were gleaming with a fierce shrewdness that Venturi had not previously detected. The wreathing smoke of Faraday's cigarette, lying in an ashtray, curled upward in fantastic shape.

"Who is Crix?"

Victor Venturi had asked the question almost unconsciously. He knew the answer now, even before he heard it from Roberts Faraday's gloating lips.

"I am Crix!" proclaimed the millionaire. "I am Crix!"

Chapter XXI

CRIX DECREES

"Fool!" The word came from the evil lips of the man who had revealed himself as Crix. "Fool! To think that you could thwart me! You have played into my hands, Venturi—into the hands of Crix!

"When Aristide Ponjeau came to America, he never dreamed that among the men with whom he talked was one who could see opportunity. He trusted all the millionaires whom he visited. He trusted Roberts Faraday among them.

"Why should I contribute two million to a fantastic dream such as Ponjeau's World Court of Industry? A great man in France—a great man at Lausanne; but Ponjeau could do nothing in world-wide affairs.

"Twenty million! Wasted millions. Easy millions. Easy for Roberts Faraday to acquire, by using his intelligence. So Roberts Faraday became Crix. How easy it was for me to learn that you represented Aristide Ponjejau in this country. I had men watching you, Venturi. But I did not stop at that; I had planned too well.

"I went to Europe—to Lausanne—and there I watched Aristide Ponjeau. Baron Hugo von Tollsburg visited him. I spied upon them. I learned their plan. A secret room aboard the dirigible *Munchen*—a hiding place for a stowaway de luxe. Von Tollsburg was to occupy it by arrangement with the commander.

"I was in that stateroom, Venturi. I had secreted myself within the berth of that room long before Von

Tollsburg arrived. When he discovered me, I choked him to death.

"The supplies that were there for him served me until we reached America. Then, using the parachute which I took aboard with me, I escaped from the dirigible unnoticed, with nothing to stop me in my plan.

Crix paused to gloat. His lips writhed in an evil smile. Venturi and Angelo were helpless before him. Crix laughed with disdain.

"Winston Collister was the first," he said. "He saw that my signature was not perfect. I killed him and took his millions. I feared a similar difficulty with Sturgis Bosworth. He was the second, and he did not question my signature. But you came there, Venturi, and I was prepared. You would never have escaped my men, but for the intervention of The Shadow.

"I have been planning since—waiting here—unsuspected. I knew that a crisis would come to-morrow night. You had disappeared—you would be here. Then came the special word that brought this previous appointment. It is you to-night, Venturi—to-morrow night, The Shadow, should he appear.

"I see your hope"—Crix laughed fiendishly as he caught a glimmer in Venturi's dark eyes—"and I can tell you that it is in vain. The Shadow, to-night? Let him come! I am ready for him. The way is blocked by a dozen men!

"You are wondering about the millions? I shall tell you where they are. Safe, Venturi, safe—in that huge vault behind me. There they will remain, Venturi, while I, posing as you, shall go with your credentials to collect from the other victims.

"I shall murder them only if I encounter trouble. Otherwise, they may live. The wealth that Ponjeau wanted will become the property of Crix. Roberts Faraday? He will merely be another of the victims."

* * *

Crix was speaking in a low, hissing tone, that carried only to Venturi's ears. The supercrook had a purpose. His announcement of his identity had been loud enough for Bart Shallock and Bumps Jaffrey to hear; these subsequent revelations were intended for Victor Venturi, alone.

"Four millions are already safe," hissed Crix. "Safe, in my impregnable vault which no cracksman could hope to enter. I am telling you all this, Venturi, because you shall not live to tell it. Your fate is sealed, Venturi, and there is nothing you can do about it.

"I am not the one who will kill you. Murder is unwise within the home of Roberts Faraday. I sent my servants way. You and your man will be taken away—by those who will dispose of you. Victor Venturi will be no more. Crix will remain.

"I have learned how you intend to notify Aristide Ponjeau that all is well. To-morrow night will be calm. Should The Shadow come here, he will find only Roberts Faraday. He will believe that Crix has given up the game.

"But after that, Crix will send the cable. As Venturi he will make collections. No trouble—no disturbance—all will be smooth for Crix. I am Crix!"

The announcement came in a louder tone. It was a reminder to the waiting men of evil that Roberts Faraday was inviolate; that the victims of the raid should be Victor Venturi and his servant, Angelo.

In terse sentences, Crix had explained the details of his game. His words had filled Venturi with despair. The Italian saw how completely he had been tricked. Nothing could stop Crix now. Most insidious of all was the fact that Venturi's death was essential to the scheme.

Never could one evil man have uncovered a surer way to immense wealth than Crix. To Roberts Faraday, a man of reputed possessions, had come tremendous opportunity, which, to nine honest men, had never suggested itself. The third upon the list of contributions to a world-wide cause, Faraday, who called himself "Crix," had plucked the ones before him, and was now planning to gather from the rest.

To Victor Venturi, there was no hope. The Italian understood the cold-blooded character of Crix. Here was a fiend who had slain others who had blocked his path. Mercy was not in Crix's quota of emotions!

"Von Tollsburg's paper are in my pocket," leered Crix, in a low tone that betokened finality. "Yours will be there soon, Venturi!"

In a loud voice, Crix uttered the single word:

"Ready!"

There was a buzz in the adjoining room. The door burst open, and in came Bart Shallock and Bumps Jaffrey. Behind them were half a dozen mobsters—Cliff Marsland amid the evil-looking crew. Each of the invaders carried a revolver. When Crix motioned with a gun toward Victor Venturi, Bumps Jaffrey walked over and poked his revolver against the Italian's ribs.

"Take the papers from him," ordered Crix. "Pass them over to me."

Bumps Jaffrey obeyed, Crix questioning him while he acted.

"You have men blocking the hall and the side door?" quizzed the master crook.

"Four of them," responded Bumps.

"Good," stated Crix. "Take these two men and give them the works. Make a sure job of it."

"Leave it to me," laughed Bumps.

Cliff Marsland faced a dilemma. Bumps Jaffrey was covering Victor Venturi and Angelo. Crix, with guns in readiness after pocketing Venturi's documents, was also a menacing figure. The other mobsters were standing in readiness.

What should Cliff do? He could start a gun fight, in an effort to save the Italians. That was his first impulse, despite the futility of the deed.

On the other hand, he could bide his time. Perhaps there would be a chance to save them; if not, would it be preferable to let them die, so that he, Cliff Marsland, could lead The Shadow to the man who was in back of all this?

Roberts Faraday, alias Crix, was a contemptible being, who plotted newer and greater crimes. Cliff knew the menace of that gloating man behind the desk. At the same time, Cliff was loath to see Venturi and Angelo die. They had been under the protection of The Shadow. Here, Cliff represented The Shadow!

Chance brought Cliff Marsland to a prompt decision. It was Victor Venturi who forced the issue. The Italian emissary, hearing his death sentence, decided upon a bold course. With a rasping cry to Angelo in his native tongue, Venturi leaped toward Bumps Jaffrey. Angelo sprang in the same direction.

Springing backward, Bumps swung his arm with deliberation. His purpose was to shoot Venturi dead. Cliff, acting spontaneously, beat the gang leader to the shot. Instinctively, Cliff fired. His bullet lodged in Jaffrey's shoulder. The gang leader dropped with a curse upon his lips.

The other mobsters leaped forward. They had taken Cliff's shot as an error of aim, for Venturi was falling upon Bumps when Cliff fired. Again, Cliff's weapon spoke, and the nearest of the surging gangsters fell. In the midst of this surprising attack, Cliff Marsland had an unexpected opportunity. There were two men, however, who caught his plan.

One was Bart Shallock; the other was Crix himself. As Cliff's second shot roared, Bart raised a gun to slay The Shadow's henchman. Crix, with quick thought, dodged away from the desk and dropped behind the end selection, raising a revolver to wing Cliff in the back.

Venturi was leaping toward Bart Shallock—too late to stop the man's aim. Angelo, seeing Crix as the chief enemy, was springing toward the desk. The mobsmen were stopped in their tracks, momentarily bewildered.

Bart Shallock's finger rested coolly on the trigger. He was pressing before Cliff could turn to fire at him. But in the excitement, not a single pair of eyes discerned what was taking place at the wall behind the desk.

The huge door of the vault was swinging outward. Beyond its moving edge appeared the head and shoulders of a sinister being. A form in black—a slouch hat drawn down above two burning eyes—a hand that held a huge-mouthed automatic. All had appeared miraculously beside that moving door.

The automatic roared. A swift messenger of death struck Bart Shallock. The confidence man sprawled forward as he fired. The bullet from his revolver splintered through the floor.

Cliff Marsland's life had been saved. A new warrior had entered the fray. The crew of evil men had encountered another foe—and the laugh that sounded through the room pealed forth the identity of this grim avenger.

It was the laugh of The Shadow!

CHAPTER XXII

THE SHADOW ANSWERS

This was the answer of The Shadow! Crix had decreed; The Shadow had replied. Crix had schemed; but The Shadow had forestalled the masquerading millionaire.

Knowing that Victor Venturi would be here to-night, awaiting the meeting that would take place between emissary and millionaire, The Shadow had entered this room before the arrival of Bumps Jaffrey's gang. He had opened the vault which Crix had boasted no one could crack; and therein he had awaited all developments.

The timely appearance of The Shadow—his unexpected arrival from the one spot that seemed impossible—these were factors that brought fear to all who saw the figure in black as it came clear of the huge swinging door.

With one shot, The Shadow had felled Bart Shallock. His second automatic was sweeping upward. Its objective was the head of Crix, peering above the end of the desk.

The fiend saw the menace. He ducked for safety. At that instant, The Shadow would have ended the career of the supercrook, but for Angelo's untimely action.

Venturi's servant, leaping forward, hurled himself across the desk and blocked The Shadow's aim just as the hand was on the trigger of the automatic.

Angelo's mad plunge took care of Crix. The Shadow saw that the Italian was overpowering the master crook, beyond the end of the desk. There were others who must be aided; Cliff Marsland and Victor Venturi; for hostile guns were covering them now.

The Shadow's automatics resounded through the room. Gangsters were his targets—evil men who fell screaming before the ferocity of his attack. Cliff Marsland pulled Venturi to the floor, and, crouching, joined The Shadow in the battle.

Turning, Cliff saw a gangster about to shoot him. Up came Cliff's revolver, to beat the mobsman to the shot. But even as Cliff pressed the trigger, he saw the gunman crumple. A bullet from The Shadow's automatic had taken care of the foe while Cliff Marsland was firing.

Bumps Jaffrey, crawling on the floor, regained his gun and swung to take a pot shot at the figure of The Shadow. Bumps was partially behind the desk; but the gleaming eyes of The Shadow discerned his skulking figure. As Bumps was rising, one automatic turned momentarily in his direction. A burst of flame and the gang leader collapsed.

Outstretched forms of mobsmen—writhing figures that seemed other than human—these were the tokens of The Shadow's fight. The answer to Crix had been a terrific attack, as effective as it was unexpected.

In rapid, roaring seconds, The Shadow had polished off this mob, so swiftly that Cliff Marsland had been scarely able to aid him. Only Crix, the master plotter, remained unscratched. He was choking on the floor, the vengeful hands of Angelo upon his neck.

A cry came from Cliff Marsland. In response, The Shadow's eyes turned toward the door. The four mobsmen stationed outside were coming in. They saw The Shadow beside the door of the safe. Their guns were swinging upward.

As The Shadow fired, his tall form swung to one side. His first bullet dropped a mobsman; then came the replying shots from the remaining trio of invaders.

They had nearly trapped The Shadow; but his action

had frustrated them. The Shadow had swung behind the half-opened door of the vault. Bullets flattened against the steel barrier. The Shadow was protected; only the muzzle of one automatic offered a target as it rested against the edge of the door.

Cliff Marsland fired at one mobsman, and wounded the fellow in the left arm. The gangster turned to fire in reply, while the others still blazed at the safe. But the muzzle of The Shadow's automatic was speaking now. It ejected swift, sure missiles toward the reinforcements who had come to aid the crippled gang.

The trio of mobsters staggered crazily. First among them was the one who had aimed at Cliff Marsland. That gangster twisted as he fell, his lips mouthing incoherent oaths. The others sprawled beside him.

A shot came from the desk. Crix, by a lucky twist, had wrested free from Angelo, and had shot the Italian with a single shot. Up came the body of the supercrook. Crix saw the shape of The Shadow emerging beyond the door of the vault.

With a cry of exultation; Crix aimed to slay the being who had been his nemesis. Cliff Marsland swung to shoot the master crook.

He could not prevent Crix from firing—Cliff was too late for that—but Cliff's sudden intervention meant that Crix would fall within a second after he delivered that single bullet toward the black-garbed form of The Shadow.

Crix had aimed with vengeance. It was too late for Cliff to save The Shadow. But the weird fighter whom Angelo had called the black ghost needed only his own firm hand to save himself. An automatic blazed from a swiftly aiming first.

The rising form of Crix poised. A strange, hideous expression covered the evil face. The outstretched hand faltered. Its fingers spread, and the revolver fell toward the floor.

Before the dropping weapon reached the woodwork,

Cliff's revolver spoke, and another bullet joined The Shadow's in the body of the supercrook.

Crix toppled with a swiftly speeding crash. He flattened motionless upon the floor. His body lay huddled, without life.

Crix, the supercrook, had been the last to die. He, like these other rats of crime, had been blotted out by The Shadow!

Victor Venturi was uninjured. The Italian, moving unsteadily, reached the form of Angelo. The servant was dying. He had been mortally wounded in his fight with Crix. Cliff Marsland went to aid Venturi; seeing that Angelo was beyond saving, Cliff stared about the room.

Everywhere were motionless mobsters. These men had sought to slay The Shadow; instead, they had met the doom which they deserved. Sure bullets had found their marks in fiends of crime; on the side of right, the only casualty was Angelo. The servant's own impetuosity had made it impossible for The Shadow to aid him and save his life.

Within a few exciting minutes, the tide had turned completely. Crix had decreed, when he had summoned his crew of mobsmen. The Shadow had answered, stepping from the vault where no one had dreamed that he could be.

Justice had triumphed over evil in this swift, exciting fight that had marked the end of the schemes evolved by Crix. The fiend and his henchmen were through.

Crix had decreed; The Shadow had answered. The triumph belong to The Shadow. The strange, sinister laugh that now echoed through the room was The Shadow's cry of victory!

Chapter XXIII

JUSTICE PREVAILS

The door to the vault lay open. The tall form of The Shadow stepped behind it. The door opened wider still. Victor Venturi looked up. Angelo was dead in the Italian's arms. Slowly, Venturi lay aside the body of his servant and rose to face The Shadow.

A now black-covered finger pointed to the interior of the vault. Venturi advanced. There, upon the floor of the vault, he saw two packages. He realized what they were. These were the packets of wealth that Crix had stolen from Winston Collister and Sturgis Bosworth.

Venturi looked toward The Shadow. He saw the gleaming eyes and stared, half in fear, half in bewilderment. The voice of The Shadow spoke, in his sinister, whispered tone.

"They are yours," were The Shadow's words. "Take them."

As Venturi reached to lift the packages, the finger pointed to a box beyond.

"That is yours, also."

In his eagerness and excitement, Venturi entirely forgot the presence of The Shadow. He carried the bundles to the desk, and opened them. Within, he found the masses of currency intact. Crix had not utilized these funds to pay Bart Shallock and Bumps Jaffrey. The supercrook had kept the millions intact.

Venturi went back to get the box which The Shadow

had indicated. He brought it to the desk—it was heavier than the packages—and opened it by a key that was in the lock. There was an envelope within. Venturi raised it, and saw a stack of money covered by a loose array of glittering gems. He recognized that these jewels possessed great value.

Within the envelope, Venturi discovered a card. It bore these words, in ink:

> Articles found within Roberts Faraday's vault. These will serve as a considerable portion of his promised contribution to Aristide Ponjeau.

Venturi closed the box. He realized that The Shadow, after opening the vault, had obtained all valuables and placed them in this one box for a definite purpose. Victor Venturi looked at the card again. The writing was disappearing letter by letter. Now, only the blank card remained!

"Are you ready?"

Looking up at the sound of the voice, Venturi saw a man in baggy trousers and sweater. It was Cliff Marsland. Venturi recognized him as the man who had stepped from the mob to start the furious battle against Crix and his henchmen. The Italian knew that Cliff Marsland was a friend.

"Yes," said Venturi. Then, looking blankly about: "Where is—where is—the one they call The Shadow?"

"He has gone," returned Cliff. "We must leave immediately. Come. There are cars outside, by the hedge. We will take one."

Victor Venturi followed Cliff Marsland's lead. The two were on their way to safety. The Shadow, his work of vengeance complete, had silently disappeared.

With Cliff aiding him in carrying the wealth that must be delivered to Aristide Ponjeau, Venturi threw a last glance back at the room, to stare at the scene of carnage which had followed Crix's vain attempt to establish crime against the wishes of The Shadow!

Police, summoned later to the home of Roberts Faraday, were confronted by a strange mystery, which was destined to enter the annals of unsolved crime. They found the body of Roberts Faraday, millionaire, surrounded by the dead forms of mobsters.

Among these was Bumps Jaffrey, a notorious gang leader. Bart Shallock, international confidence man, was also there. The body of Angelo perplexed the police. They could not learn his identity. He was obviously not a mobster.

The vault was open, and evidently it had been rifled. What had become of the men who had entered? The police did not know. They assumed that some big shots of the underworld had caused this raid; that Faraday had been forced, under threat, to open the vault.

They decided that Angelo must have been an informant who had tipped off Bart Shallock regarding some international deal on the part of Roberts Faraday. The more that the case was discussed, the more perplexing it became to the authorities.

A big shot in the offing? Strangely enough, the police did not find a clew to the name of Crix. They learned nothing regarding the double identity which Roberts Faraday had played. The body of the big shot of crime had lain before them; they had not realized it.

Weeks went by, and the strange mystery of gang war at the Faraday home was still a perplexity. But its aftermath occurred far away, in a foreign land.

At Lausanne, Aristide Ponjeau, the man of high ideals, who had planned the World Court of Industry, received from Victor Venturi the sum of nearly twenty million dollars. The contributions to the noble cause had been gathered from willing donors.

No crime had spoiled the course of these negotiations. With the death of Roberts Faraday, murder had been ended. Freed from the schemes of Crix, the great work was ready for its consummation.

Crix, the master crook! Plotter and murderer, he had planned a mad career of crime for wealth—a merciless rule of massacre and evil that had been ended by The Shadow!